G000122722

HEAD ON

HEADON

ANTHONY FOWLES

GREENWICH EXCHANGE
LONDON

This is a work of fiction and any resemblance to actual persons, living or dead, is purely co-incidental.

Greenwich Exchange, London

First published in Great Britain in 2020

Printed and bound by imprintdigital.com
Cover design: December Publications
Tel: 07951511275
Original design concept: Ellen Fowles

Greenwich Exchange Website: www.greenex.co.uk

Cataloguing in Publication Data
is available from the British Library

Cover art courtesy of Shutterstock

ISBN: 978-1-910996-40-9

to Freddy

1

HERE IT CAME AGAIN. ONCE MORE the whiteness of the A303 was streaming towards him through the big wrap-around windscreen as at a safe and sane distance behind he followed the tiny Mazda into the bright sunlight. 'Now it comes' the rational part of his brain – the part that told him even as he slept that he was dreaming – said. And now it unavoidably came. As it had originally in life the dream-time Mini detached itself from the flow of traffic speeding eastwards past his off-side and side-stepped into the central of the road's three lanes. Once again it failed to straighten. As before, as always, it continued on its diagonal path. As before, it slewed abruptly to miss the Mazda by inches and came head on straight at him.

There were those split seconds of disbelief as he stood on everything, the same glimpses of a woman, not old, not young, see-sawing her steering wheel back and forth as mindlessly frantic as a child in its first pedal car, her mouth open in the ear-splittingly silent, far-off scream forced from her by the panic in her face. Then the impact. In life, in the metal, the shock and sound had been ear-tearingly immense. The impact had slammed through bonnet and motor to shock-wave into his guts even as his truck mounted upwards and the Mini disappeared beneath its front axle. In the dream replays there was the added horror of no sound at all. But at this point, the point where the dispassionately observing part of his mind always told him he would wake up, he woke up again once more to rediscover the shadow of that original jolting body blow paining his stomach. As ever his pulse was hammering. His throat a desert.

'Jesus!' he said out loud but to no-one else, and lay there on the narrow bed in the large all-purpose room staring through the gloom at the just discernible ceiling: in a while his heartbeat would quieten and, although he would now be hours getting back to sleep, he would be calm.

Jesus ... how many more times? It must be into double figures now. Not exactly a nightmare. Not even a stress dream – the lost briefcase, the parked somewhere lorry he couldn't find – because the on-looking, recording part of his split brain was always there to tell him this was indeed a replay and not a newly recurring event. And certainly not guilt. The inquest had exonerated him completely and, more to the point, he knew in his innermost self that there was nothing he could have done, nothing he ought to have done. That poor bitch Angela Paget-Bourke had been the one and only casualty. Mrs Furbisher, the low level NHS shrink his GP had put him on to, had told him that he shouldn't reproach himself and that he felt guilty simply because of Post Traumatic Stress; because, blameless, he had survived without a single scratch ... but no ... there was more to it than that.

How many times then? Eight? Ten? Too many certainly. There was no indication it was ever going to stop ... Shit! He was wide awake now. He'd get up in a minute and have a sparrow-fart breakfast ... maybe stretch a few canvasses, a nice mechanical, distracting job ...

But why? Why did the dream keep coming back? Not guilt but something niggling. All right. It was just the start of the long summer holiday. He had time on his hands. He couldn't let this dream become the same old, same old. It was high time to get on the front front foot and see about sorting it himself.

2

AFTER THREATENING TO STOP DEAD at the first hurdle his exercise in self-help had got off to an amazingly good start. From the notes he had scribbled at the inquest he'd remembered that the copper who had outlined the routine nuts and bolts of the incident to the coroner was called Ayers. The inquest had been held in Stroud and Ayers was from the local nick. No problem sourcing the number. He put through a call.

'Police Station, Stroud.'

A woman's voice. Probably not a real copper.

'Yes, hello. I was wanting to get through to Detective Sergeant Ayers ...'

'In what regard exactly?'

'A motor accident. Any idea where he is now?'

'None at all. He's left the force. Hang on – I'll have a word.'

He heard some kind of a dull clunk. Then a diminished voice came back to him in acoustic italics.

'Anyone know where God's gift Ayers set himself up?'

Even fainter, not intelligible another voice said something on a cushion of background laughter. Then another clunk.

'Hello?'

'Yes, still here.'

'All I can tell you is Sidcup. He set up his own security business there. Don't have an address or number, I'm afraid.'

'No that's perfect. Thanks for your help.'

'You're welcome.'

'Thanks again. 'Bye.'

He switched off his mobile with an inward blaze of triumph. Sidcup! Just down the road. Of all the gin joints! No address - what else was the internet designed for?

Sidcup was indeed a right royal stroke of luck. Not only was it less than ten minutes down the road, but when you got there you could park without having to take out a second mortgage. In the event, even in his clapped-out Toyota, he did it in less than the ten minutes and was able to find a parking spot a couple of side roads off from the somewhat straggling main drag. He walked back the way he had just come. There it was right on the corner. AYERS SECURITY. Hmm, no apostrophe. But where did you ever see an apostrophe these days? Otherwise ... not bad. He stood taking the premises in.

A corner site. No over-trendy logo or clever-arse caption in sight but only the simple name above the main window and on the glass panel of the single door. The exterior paint-work on the wooden framing to the two big windows, front and side, of what would once have been a bookshop or a grocers' or a charity shop outlet was as fresh and glossy as if it had been applied the day before. And cunningly applied too – it was the same colour as a police 'phone box, Tardis blue therefore, and so a reassuring signal to every potential punter's subconscious that within there did indeed lie security and probity. He crossed the road. Closer now he could see that the big window panes were lined inside by some kind of fine metallic mesh. 'Come on in, Mr Punter. We practice what we sell.'

The front door preached the same text. It was locked but a plaque to its side asked you to press the bell. He did as he was told and with an electronic whirr of cogs and a rattle of withdrawing bolts the door automatically opened. He stepped inside and found himself in a large outer office containing two large and rather posh matching desks facing each other.

The desk to the right was unoccupied; behind the other sat the man he knew at once was the man he had come to see.

Ayers had looked up with casual curiosity as the door had opened. Now, visibly, his glance was taking on a more intense and hardening focus.

'I know you. We've met before, haven't we?'

'Yes. It was –'

'Don't tell me! Let me get there on my own ... got it! Smash-up on the A303. Inquest. You were the other driver.'

'Ten out of ten.'

'Not quite. I'm sorry but I can't do your name.'

'Shaw. Ethan Shaw'

'Of course!'

Ayer's face, decidedly puffier than it had been those three years earlier relaxed into a clearly spontaneous grin.

'How can I possibly have forgotten that,' he said. 'I was struggling with Brown or Smith. I knew it was something c –'

'Comical?'

'Commonplace – if you'll excuse me. Short. Brief and to the point.'

'My first name's not commonplace."

'No.'

'My father was a big John Wayne fan.'

'You aren't, I suppose?'

'That'll be the day. At least he didn't call me George Bernard.'

'What about this day? Now. What brings you in to see me? You moved out this way too?'

'False pretences, you'd probably have once said. I'm not a prospect for you.'

'No?'

'I am fairly local, as it happens. Up the road in Charlton. But I've only got a one bedroom flat.'

'But you've got a landlord, though.'

'I certainly have. If you've got a card, I'll gladly pass it on to her.'

'No sooner said than done. To hear is to obey,' Ayers said. He reached forward to skim a card from off the top of a stack in an open Perspex box to his right hand side.

'Here.'

Ethan Shaw stepped forward and took the business card from the outstretched hand. Ah yes, first name Ronald. Ayers he now saw was sitting in a large revolving chair that was not quite made of leather. Yes, the man had certainly put on weight since his appearance in that witness box. A good two stone at a guess. Yet he seemed to look younger now than he had then. Ah, that it was it! His hair was uniformly black. But unlike the chair's upholstery not glossy; instead it had a drab, lustreless matt look. Dyed! Ayers dyed his hair! He was fifty-something trying to come across as forty. Probably got into that practice whilst still on the force. Trust him at your peril.

'So why are you here?' Ayers was asking.

'You already flagged it up. I came about that road accident.'

'What about it?'

Concisely and truthfully Ethan Shaw told Ronnie Ayers about his recurrent problem dream.

'My shrink told me to revisit the whole thing in as much detail as possible,' he ended by saying.

Ayers frowned.

'Well, I'm afraid you've had a wasted journey coming to see me,' he said. 'I'm not equipped to get into the nitty-gritty for you. I didn't have anything to do with the vehicle forensics. They were all handled by a DI Reynolds – who was hot stuff at picking up those sort of pieces but could get tongue-tied and then stroppy in a witness box. They pushed me forward as the mouthpiece – no doubt on account of my gift of the gab and because I shine up well – but the account, all the facts, were his.'

'Oh damn!'

'Mind you, I don't see that you should be blaming yourself at all. I realise the actual crash must have been a real gut-buster for you but the reverse side of that was the CCTV footage. That being such a notorious black spot they'd not only shoved a camera up a few weeks earlier, it was actually taped up and working when it all went naughty for you. They looked at that footage all ways up and down and had to admit you didn't put a foot wrong. You weren't speeding. You were sat bang in the middle of your lane. You weren't tailgating the car in front. All good for you and lucky. If the footage hadn't been there in black and white, what with you being so young the brief might have given you a hard time. But seeing's believing. No way it was down to you.'

'Thanks,' Ethan Shaw said. 'This Reynolds – where would I find him?'

Ayers shrugged his heavy shoulders. There was a second chin thickening up around his neck.

'Anyone's guess,' he said. 'He was at Cheltenham in those days. Seconded to us because it was such a high profile incident.'

'What? The wife of an MP being involved and all that?'

'Exactly. Lots of publicity ... the powers that be slammed in their top man. I've an idea Reynolds has moved on from the force as well since then.'

'Ah well,' Ethan Shaw said. 'What caused you to switch yourself then?'

Ayers pulled his mouth across his pawky chops to manufacture a wry grin.

'One promotion application too many rejected,' he said.

'And why come here?'

'Ah. Leafy South East London, leafier inner Kent. Lots of folk in these parts who like to think they're comfortable. Nice homes, Audi outside. They all vote Conservative, they're all dedicated to keeping what's theirs theirs. And shit scared of losing it. They go on cruises. They love off-gefucking sur le continent. Puts them one up on their neighbours. Only they feel terrified all the time they're away on their jolly old hols that when they get back home they'll find the place ransacked.'

'Which is where you come in.'

'Right. I've got a locksmith here who can open everything or keep it shut to anyone else. I've got an electronics whizz-kid and his team who can do ditto their way.'

'So what do you do yourself?'

'When a prospect comes through the door I go back to his place and talking like a Dutch uncle recce his set up. If it's a domestic that's easy, I admit, because although they don't know it they all live in the same home. Lately, mind you, I'm pleased to say, we've started expanding into industrial premises. That's where the real money is. Ironic fact is that all those early retirements from the Kent police have pushed up the crime rate and the good citizens' anxiety levels that little bit more than they can bear. More grist to my mill.'

You fat, complacent slug, Ethan Shaw thought.

'I should have thought that only pushed up the crime rate on the Costa Brava,' he said.

He saw Ayers frown.

'Well, I'm sorry to have been a waste of your time,' Ethan Shaw lied, 'I think you're right.'

'I should let it rest,' he lied again, 'I imagine I will.'

'No problem,' Ayers said on automatic pilot. 'You do that.'

He made a studied show of reaching for a file and taking out a document. Ethan Shawn could take a hint.

Turning on his heel he left Ayers alone in his Tardis blue heaven.

Eight minutes going, nine coming back: he was returned to his flat well before lunch time. He had a microwave-warmed coffee and then, checking that the post was no more than junk mail, suited his action to the hour by whipping up a plain two egg omelette. It was only as he was washing up the frying pan and the single plate that it came home to him that the rest of the day, afternoon and evening, stretched away before him entirely empty. Well, the devil made work for idle hands. He still had his degree to worry about. Gathering up his sketch book, his pencil and charcoal kit, he headed for the door. One bus ride would get him to Greenwich.

In due slow course he was getting off the bus around the corner from the Cutty Sark. He made for the splendid lift which dropped down to the pedestrian tunnel under the Thames and, fighting off the aura of Jack the Ripper Victorian horror that pervaded its long length, walked through to the tunnel's matching lift sunk into the river's northern bank. Within seconds he was into the small, pleasant park on the southernmost tip of the Isle of Dogs. He found a place to sit and stared across the river at the view.

He was aware it was a cliché viewpoint. As near as dammit it was the identical spot which had been picked out some two hundred and fifty years previously by Canaletto and by pretty much every halfways competent amateur artist in the world ever since. But that made the challenge even more interesting. The thing was to contrast the four-square neo-classical buildings of the Queen's House and of what had once been the Royal Naval College with the free flowing Thames in the foreground and the similarly fluid rise of the green hill up beyond the solid buildings to the distant Observatory at the top. He would cheat on the hill by adding more trees. Because the sky was overcast the light was even and soft but beneath a higher grey layer ominously dark clusters of cloud were hanging motionlessly, it seemed, over the entire scene. It would have been child's play to capture this effect in water colours and maybe he should come back some time to do just that but meanwhile the challenge was, well, challenging. At the very worst a sketch might well serve as his starter for 10. He set to work.

For a while he was lost in what he was trying to do. The basic perspective was not quite as simple as first met the eye then, a particularly melodramatic cloud formation capping the hill, he thought to take a photograph for future reference. At the very point he was taking out his smart phone luck came his way. Into view on his left came a Thames sailing barge beating up against the current on the in-flowing tide. He snapped that as well and studied the instant image. Now he really wished he had colour to work with. The nobly utilitarian triangle of the barge's dull red-brown main sail was a splendid punctuation mark on the riverscape. Still, he had the colour reference now. He must definitely come back armed to the teeth. Yes, the barge in the foreground couldn't help but diminish the receding view but the dramatic triangle of the sail would emphasise the rectangularity of the buildings behind. Thus he would be able to infiltrate beneath the 18th-century subject a subconscious hint of 20th-century cubism. In fact, come to think of it now, he was thinking of it, for those with an eye to see it, the contrast between barge and background nicely pointed the difference between the toilers of the sea and the toffs who lived across the water. Turner, of course would have seen all that at once without the real-life prompt.

He reached for his eraser, and, studying the photographic image, spent time working the barge into the foreground composition. Then a fat splat of rain fell on to his sketching pad. He closed it up at once. Time to go home. His eyes were dazzling anyway, his wrist tightening up. Quit while you're ahead. The same bus took him home and en route he decided to beguile the evening time by cooking something semi-ambitious. He didn't really have the ingredients to be that elaborate and since he had some ready-made pastry settled for a steak and kidney pie that would stretch to a second meal later in the week. It turned out to look quite like the picture in the recipe book. Then, after he had finished the day's second bout of washing up, he did what he had always aimed to do that evening. He put the name of Hilary Paget-Bourke into his laptop's search engine. The entry had been significantly altered since the time of the inquest, nearly three years ago, when he'd last been there. It outlined what he'd remembered, what you'd expect. Eton, Balliol ... yes, par for the course. President of the Oxford Union – high flyer, then. But no! – Only a third class degree (scraped at that, if gossip column memory served). But, look, 'explained' in a verbatim quotation 'I'm afraid that in my last year I succumbed to a combination of sloth and networking!' You bet you did, you lazy sod. Your father an old bruiser Conservative cabinet minister, you wouldn't think being at Oxford had anything to do with studying or with trying to master a subject, would you now? What else? Yes, himself an MP – for the constituency of Birchfield – since three general elections ago; the first of which saw him the youngest MP in the House. Him and Pitt the Younger. Latterly, his father now dead, a Parliamentary Private Secretary in his own right. Then, tacked on the new data. First his marital status; widower. Just that. No name, no pack drill. Far more copy was devoted to what the widowered world and his wife knew all about anyway. The dramatic resignation of his role as a Conservative PPS. As a Conservative indeed. The entry wrote up his dramatic 'crossing of the floor' not to join with Labour (of course not!); not even to link up with the Lib-Dems; but so as to represent in the House a new party that he had formed out of the ruins left by UKIP's collapse. The Independent National Party. Oh, he'd played the white man. Faced with uproar from some of his constituents he'd resigned his seat and fought the ensuing bye-election as an In Party candidate. He'd judged it nicely. Although his majority was reduced from thousands to hundreds, his work as a local MP, the frequency of his hits on television interviews, *Have I Got News For You?*, his famous glamorous charm had seen him returned again. Now, the summary concluded, he was a party leader – leader of a party of two. Within a month Rupert Caldicot, the erstwhile Cornish Tory MP had followed an identical path. Ethan Shaw shut down his laptop. Hmm ... So, give or take a bit,

Hilary Paget-Bourke was the type to whom Ronnie Ayers might well end up selling a security system.

Well, you never knew. A couple more seats at Westminster (not impossible) then with neck and neck Socialists and Tories heading for a maybe hung parliament, the new IN Party might make all the difference. Yes, Hilary Paget-Bourke might conceivably become a power broker at that.

3

IF SIDCUP HAD BEEN A DODDLE Birchfield was a right bummer. Lying almost due west of London – the dot-on-the-map village necessitated a slog right across the city for anyone stupid enough to set out from Charlton. He had considered the trains but the service to the obvious country halt was as disjointed as the cost was exorbitant. There was nothing for it but to get up at the crack of dawn and cross London while the bus lanes were still up for grabs. Sleeping badly – but not dreaming that dream – he was nevertheless up with the alarm and on the road well before seven.

It never ceased to amaze him on such early-start occasions how many people going in to their nine to fives started their day at six. But although thick on the road, the traffic was moving and he was through to London's western side before the bus lanes became no-go areas. When he picked up the 303 just past Oxford it came to him that this was the first time he had driven the route since the crash.

Because of the wheezing, fluffy-engined Toyota he made no play to overtake when the 303's notorious alternating central lane gave priority to westbound drivers. He tooled along at a rigorously frugal 55. Quite early at this stage, he found his gut churning and tightening at the thought that in a while, soon, right now, curse it, he was going to go through his own personal black spot.

In the event though, probably because of the huge difference in viewpoint between the low-slung Toyota and the lorry's elevated cabin, he was almost past the few fatal yards of the head-on smash before he recognised as much. It wasn't at all the dream. Nor was there any point in stopping, even if he could have. A few minutes later he was turning into the first of the network of B roads that would take him to Birchfield.

Now he was in the country proper. Two approaching cars could hardly pass each other here and he needed to keep an eye on the sustained ditches ribboning along just beyond his on-side front. But no-one else was about and suddenly the burgeoning hedges thrusting out to further threaten his vehicle's parti-coloured body-work had dwindled away and he was driving past a modernist school whose playground was filled with tinies rampaging through their mid-morning break. Three or four houses set back at an expensive distance from the road and, bingo, he was slowing down as he entered the untidy, irregular, local version of a village square. There was a mini-parade of shops along one side but the area was dominated by a pub at the further end of the build-up and, at right angles to The Fox, the garage, a bare three pumps on its forecourt, which he was looking for. Mitchell was the name his inquest notes had told him.

He needed to fill up in any case. He cruised alongside the Ordinary pump and, gritting his pauper's teeth, did exactly that. He went on into the office section to pay. Glass and steel and plastic – it was surprisingly contemporary for its surroundings. Still the site did pump out a national brand of petrol. This glorified portacabin must be their starter-for-ten down-market set-up for low level outlets in the sticks.

'£30.82.' The girl behind the counter with its top dressing of cheap confectionary said in an accent that definitely did not come from London. Quite pretty really. Probably hated her hum-drum lot. Along with his credit card he fished out his number one chat up smile.

'Mr Mitchell about?' he said.

Without hesitation the girl jerked her head sideways.

'In the workshop round the back if you want to talk to him,' she said.

'Just a quick word,' he answered.

'You'll have to go back outside and then go around ...'

'Right. Thanks.'

The rear office – if there was one – must be off-limits to peasants like himself. Well, she had her orders. Not her fault. He went quickly out to the forecourt and eased his Toyota forward from the pumps into the lee of two fifth-hand old-model Fords that were being offered for sale at knock-down prices. Obediently he made his way round towards the workshop in the back.

Ah, there. Behind the pop-up fronting cabin stood a quite large brick building perhaps a hundred and fifty years old. A stable maybe once. It had a large double doored entry and through the open leaves came the repeating sound of metal clanking. He went through the wide opening and as his eyes adjusted to the dank shadow within saw an ageing Vauxhall Cresta raised high on a hoist. Crouched underneath the car a man in overalls seemed to be doing something to its exhaust.

'Mr Mitchell?' he said loudly.

The man stopped hammering and ducking out from under the car's chassis came forward to meet him.

Now history repeated itself. The man's initial curiosity hardened into recognition and then into a quite obvious unwelcoming further awareness. Once again Ethan Shaw found himself explaining his quite genuine concern over his recurrent dream-interrupted sleep patterns. As he spoke he took stock.

Mitchell was a tall, sandy looking fellow with a tired, sad featureless face. A potato face whose puffiness had not kept the mesh of wrinkles from around his pale eyes and his small tight mouth, at bay. He had lost the fronting half of his thinning, pale hair from off his skull but didn't seem at all the type to make a virtue of the resulting village simpleton effect by shaving his entire scalp fashionably bald. He was listening to Ethan Shaw's tale with all due attention.

'Well I'm sorry it's caught up with you like,' he said at last. 'It must have been horrible, no question. But believe me you're not the only one to suffer consequences.'

His accent was identical to the girl's. Father and daughter.

'All the same,' Mitchell went on, 'I don't think I can help you.'

'It's just that there's this huge discrepancy,' Ethan Shaw said. 'Huge – but the inquest never went into it.'

'What's that?'

'The police team put the accident down to a malfunctioning steering box. The key central lynch-pin bolt just wasn't there. But the car had an up to date MOT certificate ...'

'That's right. It did ... Still had about six months to go on it.'

'Did you issue the certificate?'

Mitchell let out a wan, an almost despairing, sigh of a breath.

'Not me,' he said. 'I can't run to that sort of kit in here. Nor is there enough trade locally for MOT work. But I did take that car in for its test certificate. Here's how it used to work. Mrs Paget-Bourke, usually, would bring any of the cars up there in Buckingham Palace whose MOT was running out in to me for a full service. Then for an extra hour of my work's time, she'd have me run the vehicle into Simpson's in Stroud and get a new certificate there.'

'And that's what happened with the Mini?'

'Yes.'

'So did you service it first?'

'Yes. And there was nothing wrong with the steering box then. Nothing at all. I mean, page one – as soon as you got the car up on the hoist you automatically check the steering. And I did that then and all myself. I ran to an apprentice in those days – a good lad, knew his stuff. But I wasn't going to put my connection with my number one customer at any kind of risk.. That Mini was all snug and tight. Big standard central bolt, nut, washers, locking nut. The lot. I mean I drove it into Stroud and back after servicing it and she went like a bird.'

'But you say you suffered consequences afterwards ...'

Mitchell gave the helpless shrug of a man way over his head into something he would never get to cope with.

'What do you think?' he said. 'After that verdict do you think I ever got any more work from Buckingham Palace, the Paget-Bourkes? Not a sniff of anything – and up to then they had been my banker. Not only that but Lord Lah-di-dah started putting the word around. I'll swear to it. Other regulars stopped bringing their vehicles in. Work all but dried up. He's got a lot of respect round here, if not from me. Work's never picked up enough since.'

'Who gets to do it now?'

'Hah!' Mitchell let out a snort of total disgust and disaffection. 'Lord Lah-di-dah now has his own chauffeur, minder and head-cook-and-bottle-washer, doesn't he? That sodding Reynolds does the maintenance stuff for him now, and if it's major, takes it God knows where.'

'Who? Who does it now?'

'Reynolds as above. Don't know his first name. Used to be a copper. Sitting pretty now up there in the Palace.'

Ethan Shaw worked at keeping his face expressionless as something in his mind moved sideways at this new intelligence.

'This Buckingham Palace as you keep calling it,' he said. 'What's its real name?'

'Birchfield Hall.'

'Where is it?'

'Go out of here, pass The Fox on your left, follow the road out. It's about a mile on from there. You can't miss it.'

'Right. Close then.'

'Too bloody close.'

'Well OK. Seems I shouldn't be losing my beauty sleep at that after all. Thanks for your time. I shouldn't be taking up any more of it.'

'No more you should.'

All right, Ethan Shaw thought, don't have a nice day then. Nodding he turned and walked back to his car and for a long minute sat motionless in it thinking. The village 'square' was no more than a widening of the B road that had brought him there. Opposite The Fox was the mildewed-looking bronzish statue of some gink in a Victorian frock coat. It seemed to sum up the place. To sum up Mitchell. Come on now! Think! Yes, why not? It was madness after having driven so far on this flimsy muddle-headed wild goose chase not to go that extra mile. He wouldn't want to have to do it a second time, would he? He turned the ignition key and edged out on to the road proper and following it cruised past the pub.

The hedge rows closed in claustrophobically. Abruptly they were replaced on his left by a mellow red-bricked wall. Then came a space – the opening caused by the leaves of a wide iron gate set fully apart either side of a driveway. Clearly the entrance to Birchfield Hall. Nothing behind him. He braked to a full stop.

He found himself uncharacteristically embarrassed. If Hilary Paget-Bourke was such the Lord Lah-di-dah that Mitchell maintained he didn't want to tool up that drive-way in his parti-coloured heap of an old wreck. The matt black bonnet and offside wing would not create a level playing field for any dialogue that might develop. He put the Toyota in motion again and two hundred yards further along found a verge of sorts where he might park. He walked back and turning through the gate, as far again towards the house to which the drive-way lead.

It was clearly a gem. Fairly small. What? Twelve bedrooms, say – the shape and proportions of a Palladian house executed in Queen Ann-ish red brick. It had a gently sloped slate roof so that, miniaturised, it would have made a perfectly understated tea caddy. What made it seem so perfectly balanced was the positioning of the front door. Modestly small, it was smack bang centre of the flat-windowed frontage. The symmetry it emphasised was total.

As was his luck. Set back from the house towards the left side as he approached was a second building. Like Mitchell's workshop it had clearly once been stables. Now it too served as a garage for cars. And right now as he advanced a man in dungarees was working hard and fast at delivering a chamois-leathered finish to a new-model Jaguar saloon. He looked every inch an ex-copper. Ethan Shaw walked straight towards him.

'Mr Reynolds?' he asked.

'Who wants to know?' the man said without looking up from his wiping down.

'Oh, I'm sorry. We haven't quite met. My name's Ethan Shaw.'

'Quite met?' Still the polishing continued.

'That head on crash on the 303 you worked on some years ago - I was the other driver.'

'Oh yeah,' Reynolds said. 'I thought the name rang a bell.'

For the first time Reynolds stood up and stared at him directly.

'And so?' he said.

Yet again Ethan Shaw found himself going through what increasingly if illogically he was beginning to think of as his cover story. Reynolds listened to him in a stony-faced silence exactly as if he were a long experienced policeman hearing a pathetically invented alibi from a frequently guilty suspect. He was a man of medium height whose short pudding basined and parted hair served to emphasise the roundness of his head and features. He had dark, suspicious eyes. He looked solid rather than plump. Now at last he was wringing out the chamois leather.

'No skin off your nose,' he adjudicated. 'You came out of it smelling like a rose.'

He tossed the leather into a bucket.

'No need to get your knickers in a twist at all,' he said.

'My shrink says it's because deep down I feel guilty I survived,' Ethan Shaw said.

'Tell yourself that some you win some you lose,' Reynolds said. 'That's life, not you.'

'I made the mistake of crawling down underneath afterwards. You know, just to see if by some miracle she was still living.'

Reynolds advanced a step forward.

'Yeah,' he said. 'A big mistake. Blood and glass all over. And paste. I've been there in my time. Look maybe it's your brain telling you to wake up before you come to the really nasty bit.'

'I can remember that bit only too much all by myself, thank you very much.'

'Yeah. When our team worked on the reconstruction the first thing we had to do was hosepipe the last traces of her away.'

'Ugh. You found the lynch-pin to the steering box was missing, didn't you?'

'Not there. Not a trace. Never found it. When it hit you that car was pigeon toed.'

'Only it did have an MOT. Mitchell swears it was there, locking nut stock and washer, the last time he serviced it.'

Reynolds pulled a look of contempt across his tough fat face.

'That cowboy loser,' he said. 'Well he would say that, wouldn't he? Been talking to him then, have you?'

'Yes. I thought –'

'Everyone knows he doesn't know his trade. Doubt if he knows one end of a monkey wrench from another. He'll be out of business and bankrupt six months from now.'

'All the same.'

'All the same, my arse. He's probably the one left the locking nut off. Rushing the job to get on with the next one. No one to help him, you see. Locking nut off the first nut would vibrate loose wouldn't it? You're left with just the bolt holding it all together. Then all you need is a speed bump or, round here a pothole, more like, to flip the bolt out. We searched the last route she drove inch by inch all the way back to here. The last time she took that Mini out it was no safer than a Mercedes in a Paris underpass.'

Bastard, Ethan Shaw thought.

'So,' Reynolds said brusquely. 'Who sic'd you on to us, then? The sister?'

'Mitchell. I don't think he votes for your boss.'

'He's always had a loose mouth.'

'Well, if he is the villain of the piece I can rest easy. Seems like he's going to get his just deserts anyway.'

And I'm a bastard too, he thought.

'I used to have trouble sleeping after seeing certain things I did see when I was first on the force,' Reynolds said. 'You're never quite prepared for the next one. I reckon that's why I fetched up here.'

He looked at Ethan Shaw with a suddenly increased shrewdness.

'How'd you get here today?' he said.

'Train,' Ethan Shaw said at once. 'Walked from Birchfield. That pub, The Fox – any good for food?'

'It's all right if you're hungry. Take you all hours hanging about to get back.'

'Don't I know it.'

''Tell you what – there's a short cut to Birchfield. Go down the drive. Just opposite the gates – well, slightly to the left – there's a gap in the hedge and a stile. Over the stile there's a bridle path. The field there belongs to us. But the path's anyone's. It'll bring you out bang at The Fox.'

'Oh, right. Thanks. I've got all day but I'll take it.'

'You'll be doing yourself a favour. Just as you will if you put all that's been right out of your mind.'

'Yes. Thanks. Sorry to have broken into your day.'

'No problem.'

'Nice meeting you.'

Or not. Ethan Shaw walked back down the drive. It was, he

discovered now that he thought about it, a beautiful summer's morning. The grass was green, the sky was blue and the birds were firing off shrill warning signals at the sight and sound of him. What was the word ... Bucolic? Yes, that was it. Like in a fairy tale. Hansel and Gretel. Little Red Riding Hood. Sunny skies, balmy breezes then wham! Lost in the wood and a grim old Grimm outlook. No. Nonsense. Why should he think like that? It would always have been Reynold's stock in trade to come over as malevolent as that.

He had reached the iron gate at the end of the drive. Yes, sure enough, there across the public road diagonally to the left was a stile set in front of the fronting hedgerow. Sinister, indeed. Why did he inescapably feel it masked a machine-gun nest, barrels trained on him? Come on now! Don't be ridiculous. Keep calm and carry on. He walked over to the stile, climbed up onto the lower step and took a look at what he could see. A field. Quite large: about a hundred yards wide ahead of him and two hundred off to his left. The stile was in what you might call the top corner. Immediately to its right was a second hedge running at a right angle to the one bordering the road. And, sure enough, a signpost and a beaten flat path running alongside this second hedge to disappear into a thick copse – no, call it a wood – that hundred yards or so straight ahead. Apart from the path the field was all grass and quite lush and high grass at that. At its distant, further end a small group of cows stood placidly chewing the cud ignoring or oblivious of him. Blue skies, green grass, a herd of cows – a quintessential English scene. Too flat, too commonplace to paint. But dangerous?

He had, he discovered thrown a leg over the stile's top bar and had stepped-jumped down into the field at the near end of the footpath. He did not set off down it. Instead, looking to the road-side hedge to his left, he picked out an interruption in its long length. About thirty yards down a tree thrust up to break the hedge's uniform height. He made for that. Yes, good, around the base of the tree trunk there was an irregular circle of space. Amused now by the ridiculous extremes to which he was going he edged into the space and crouched down behind the tree. He began to wait.

Minutes passed. Nothing. He began to feel a complete and utter prat. He looked at his watch. He would give it another minute. The minute was gone. He was about to rise up on his feet when there was another chatter of look-out birds. He darted back down again. There was a scraping sound and then a man's voice said something he couldn't catch.

There came a series of thumps and, as he scrunched down even lower, two men appeared in the field. One was Reynolds. He no longer wore overalls but a tweedy jacket with lots of leather patches and corduroy trousers stuffed into boots that laced halfway up his shins. After him appeared a second man wearing a dark green Barbour jacket. He was slim but a good half a head taller than Reynolds and his own head was topped by fair hair that positively gleamed in the sun. It was three years since he had seen him at the inquest but he recognised him at once. Hilary Paget-Bourke. Even as he clocked him again at this hidden distance, Ethan Shaw found himself taking in a short sharp breath. Reynolds was half turning to speak to his boss.

'He's no slow-coach,' Ethan Shaw heard Reynolds say.

He only half-heard that. His own release of breath had almost masked the sound. What had caused him to gasp was that, as he had turned to face Paget-Bourke, Reynolds had revealed that under his right arm he was carrying a twin- bore shotgun.

'We'll press on,' the cultured and familiar from television voice replied. 'We know he can't get too far.'

As Ethan Shaw continued to watch, the two men strode towards the distant copse. His heart beating fast, he saw them go on. When they had become lost in the far trees he moved swiftly back to the stile and hopping over it as quickly as he could, scrambled back into the road. He heard no cries from behind. No machine gun or shotgun whizzed a death song past his ears.

Still the sun shone. Quintessential England! He walked as fast as possible to where he had parked his car. It seemed to be unscathed. He turned the ignition key, drove a few yards testing the steering. It seemed to be fine. Not entirely logically he felt safe and secure now that he was back in his own vehicle.

Letting the engine idle he took the time to go over his jumbled thoughts. What had he seen? Had he seen that? Yes, of course he had. And seeing was believing. But impossible to believe. In broad daylight? Right on their own doorstep? Impossible. It wasn't August yet, if that was relevant. It had to be coincidence. But again: 'We know he can't get far.' That wasn't chance. Hmm ... food for further thought or what! Well, time to join the wise men's club. Setting the Toyota in motion he began his return home by another way.

4

USUALLY WHEN HE DROVE LONG DISTANCES Ethan Shaw would end the trip too hollowed out to feel hungry. This time, however, when he got back to South London, he was feeling ravenous.

Partly, no doubt, this was due to his having kept on eastwards through the usual lunch-hour so as to take advantage of the consequently comparatively thinned-out traffic. Partly, dwelling on the extraordinary coda to his Birchfield visit must have driven all thought of food from his mind. It was extraordinary! It had been the everyday familiarity with which Reynolds had been toting that shotgun, he finally decided, that had made that pastoral walk in the sun seem so menacing. But if so everyday, why the menace? Once again, broad daylight, the inevitable noise, Paget-Bourke at his side ... The far-fetched very enormity of what had gone through his thoughts had to rule out such a melodramatic scenario. The game could never have been worth their candle. But, then again, seeing was believing. Was he fetching it from so very far after all?

When eventually he came to the Wandsworth one-way system a nasty pile-up, as he belatedly discovered, had caused virtually wholesale gridlock. Foreground irritation and the need to improvise a way through when there wasn't one drove all other musings out of his head. When at last he did get through, the

Old Kent Road was bumper to bumper. He drew up at last outside his flat exhausted and, he now found, starving. His chaotic studio flat seemed strangely claustrophobic on his return. The roads he had travelled were still streaming through his brain. With his nerves still twitching he hadn't the energy to cook. Even though money – the lack of it rather – was starting to be a problem again he decided to splurge. Early, he went out again to eat in the Percival Arms. There wasn't much that was gastro about its food but, not being able to offer quality, the governor there did err on the side of quantity. Friday night, of course. Already the place was heaving. But they managed to squeeze him in and three pints and the cottage pie later, he had taken enough on board to feel no more than sated and dog-tired despite the non-stop babble surrounding him. Once more it was a downer to be alone among all such bright-eyed and bushy-tailed chumminess but the food and drink had given him a means of avoiding his own isolation. He walked back home and went to bed straight away. The roads were out of his head now. He slept like a top.

When he awoke his head was clear. The week-end. Well, students didn't lead a Monday to Friday existence. He still had the portrait to contend with. He'd try and finish it once and for all. He hadn't had his documentary nightmare. Perhaps revisiting – however briefly in passing – its real-life location had exorcised it. The wild goose chase had served its turn. Now he would forget that too.

He made toast and fresh coffee and crossing to the plastic-covered floor space that defined the 'studio' area of his big one room put the portrait on his easel again. A self-portrait. It was a mandatory requirement of his degree course and at the end of the coming term he would have to hand it in. He considered it now and his heart sank. Two weeks after he had last fooled with it, his appraisal was fresh once more. Alas. No, he didn't like it. Now it was all but finished, he could tell it wasn't working.

It was a good likeness, yes, but in the same way a passport

photo was a likeness. It was flat and superficial – a likeness, yes, but not the true him. Could he redeem it by replacing the indeterminate background wash with something specific? Bookshelves perhaps? A corner of this very studio? No. That would fool nobody. Such a cheap trick with background fuss would detract from the portrait itself. And he couldn't presume to copy Chardin or Rembrandt.

His own realistic image stared sullenly back at him offering no help. He retreated as far from it as the room allowed, but no ... distance brought neither enchantment or illumination. A goodish-looking face, yes, dark, symmetrical, good cheekbones, but no soul. Perhaps working in oil had cramped his style.

Dammit all that time expended on nothing! He'd have to start again from scratch, try for something looser. Watercolour might indeed be the answer but he was damned if he would work in acrylic ... Oh hell! ... today's vibes weren't right. Leave it for now.

Leaving the misfire on the easel he set about assembling his outdoor kit. He'd go back to the Isle of Dogs and work on his previous homage to (or rip-off of) Canaletto and Cezanne.

Here it came again. In the middle of the night the rational, registering part of his brain in the middle of his head was telling him that, no, his wild goose travels had all been for nothing. Once more the roadscape was streaming towards him through the wide windscreen of his lorry's high cabin. There was the Micra up ahead where it always was. Here, yes, but please no, came the Mini skittering insanely into the central lane. Again the documentary re-run showed him the terrified see-sawing driver uncontrollably hurtling ever closer. Again as she disappeared beneath his overhanging vision he heard the stomach-turning violence of the silent crunch as his cabin bucked upwards. And now ... he did not wake up.

Instead the film had jump-cut. He was down on all fours the road surface hard upon his knees as he ducked forward to see if there was any chance the woman had survived. No! Don't go there! To have seen it once was to remember it for a lifetime. Too late! Paste.

Shuddering upward, he hurtled awake. Chest heaving, pulse racing, panting in thick fast bursts he was sitting up in bed. Darkness. Not yet daybreak. But here he was in bed. He was all right. No exorcism had occurred but he was alive and well.

He lay back down and as his pulse and breathing slowed stared up at the distant, hazy ceiling. This usually worked. By the time his eyes had adjusted and he could make out the scraggly brush strokes on the foxed plaster overhead he would be over this latest insult to his system. Time passed. The dimness brightened. Gradually he sensed he was breathing normally.

'Who sic'd you onto us? The sister?'

As unbidden as the recurring nightmare the voice, an alien voice, had sounded echoingly inside his skull. Reynolds' voice! Ye gods! He had let that remark go by him! He never should have! It was a huge bonus! Reynolds had tipped his hand. There was, of course, a sister. She had been there at the inquest.

He had only the faintest memory. She had not been required to testify. She had sat at the back. Alone. In an appropriate black coat, he seemed to remember. No more than a smudge now on his recollection. Little more than. Well, he'd had more than enough on his plate to keep him busy at the time. But of course she had a name. Would she still have it? The same obviously as Paget-Bourke's dead wife's maiden name. What the hell had it been?

For perhaps a good hour he lay trying to bring the name back to mind. He'd heard it certainly ... something upmarket as you'd expect. Posh. Come on now, think! But it wouldn't come. He tried forcing his brain to think. He tried creeping up on it by picking his England team to play Mars? Gascoyne? No. That sort of thing, though. But no ... Well, tomorrow was another day. He'd go look it up.

He rolled on to his side. It still wanted a while before full daylight. He should try for a bit more shut-eye. The replay never came twice in a night. He closed his eyes and a new thought came. This time of his own making.

His wild goose chase had been no such thing! He'd been right on the button! That stroll across the green and pleasant meadow had not been an everyday story of simple country folk. OK you couldn't make it up but that was no reason to give the pair the benefit of a doubt that wasn't there in the first place. They'd been gunning for him. Maybe just to throw a scare into him. But it had been there. Waiting to happen. A man carrying a gun across a field had only one intention – to put it to some use. Broad daylight or not. Well, he would have to think about that. Do something about it.

Once more he felt his heart beating faster. This time it felt good.

Fronting the lower road through from Greenwich to Woolwich stood the four-square Edwardian-built main Borough Library. He knew the reference section well. While he had used his laptop in the main, to bone up on the Bellini's and Titian's which the Art History part of his course required him to take in, he had spent hours in the reference section reading more generally as he strove to plug some of the huge gaps his ramshackle education had inflicted on his knowledge. He knew for certain there were volumes of *Who's Who* on the shelves there. Within seconds of taking the most recent to a table he had the name. Faulkner. Of course! Hilary Paget-Bourke had married Angela Faulkner, elder daughter of Edward and Lilian Faulkner.

He turned to the capital F in the F pages. Nothing. But there was a *Who Was Who* further along the shelf and yes, another bullseye.

Edward Faulkner, CBE. (1959-2014) Chemical engineer. CEO Faulkner Metals (1990-2012) m. Lilian Metcalfe (1979-): daughters Angela (1980), Virginia (1992).

Hmmm ... the library, he knew, was a repository for all the phone directories dedicated to Greater London. What were the odds? Long and faint, no doubt. Nevertheless. He crossed to the appropriate shelves and, at considerable length, found the four volumes of the old A-Z set. The second one therefore. Hmmn ... Nine listings under Faulkner when spelt that way. But – would you believe it! The last in line was a Ms V. Faulkner at a Hammersmith address. It would be worth a call for starters. He scribbled the name down.

Not too late that evening he duly made the call. He began assembling his thoughts to compose the answer machine message he would doubtless be required to leave. But no. Surprising him by the promptness the call was answered directly.

'0244.'

Zero and not O. What did that indicate?

'Er ... good evening. I was hoping to get in touch with a Virginia Faulkner.'

'You've succeeded. Speaking.'

A BBC-ish voice. Cool, calm and collected to the point of severity.

'Ah ...'

'May I ask your name?'

'My name won't mean anything to you. We haven't met. It's Shaw. Ethan Shaw.'

'Actually your name does ring a rather loud bell. It's not that hard a one to remember is it?'

'Well, as I'm always telling people, my father liked Westerns.'

'You're the man my sister drove into, aren't you?'

He let out his breath as his pulse quickened.

'I'm so glad you put it that way,' he said. 'I've no wish to open old scars.'

'Rather fresh scars, actually. But don't worry. I can talk about it these days. I was at the inquest, of course.'

'Yes.'

'I remember you from there. I came expecting to loathe you,

but I was rather impressed by the way you gave evidence. Thank you, by the way, for expressing your sympathy – the Coroner apart, nobody else did.'

'Well…'

''What can I do for you now?'

Was it wishful thinking but had her voice lost its sharper edge?

'Talk about all that, if you can bear it.'

'Why should I want to do that?'

Once again he was committed to his set piece. He described his problem sleeping, the nature of his nightmare.

'Par for the course I should have thought these days,' she said at last. 'Are you seeing anyone about it?'

'I did. But not anyone whose was really grown-up or, indeed, effective.'

'What makes you think I'm grown-up?'

'There's a bit more to it now, I think.'

'Oh?'

'I've tried exorcising, getting rid of–'

'I know what exorcising means.'

'I've been revisiting the scene of the crash. Asking questions. I met the copper, ex-copper now, who headed up the crash investigation.'

'Did you now?'

'Yes. Didn't like him. He didn't like me. He's working for your former brother-in-law now.'

What he heard down the line was a gasp of wholesale surprise.

'Is he now?!'

'Yes. Look – I know it will sound far-fetched but I'm coming to think that what happened is not an accident pure and simple.'

'What… Sabotage?'

'Yes. And if it was, then it was murder too.'

He had come on too strong, got there too fast. She hadn't rung off but there was nothing down the line but silence.

'Hello?' he said.

'Sorry, I was thinking ... You know it might be an idea at that if you and I were to meet.'

'That's why I rang. It was just what I was going to propose.'

'I'm in Hammersmith.'

'I worked that out from the post code.'

'I'm only a few minute's walk from the main drag there, King Street.'

'I know it.'

'There's a half-ways good Italian restaurant down the far end of King Street – the Bella Vista.'

'Right.'

'Could we meet there tomorrow?

'Yes. It's a bit of a shlep for me. I'm over in South East London; but, yes, fine. What else are oyster cards for?'

'I'll book a table for 7.30. It's straight on down from the tube station on the one way system. A long five minutes walk.'

'As long as it's not six.'

'Right. I'll see you then and there. Don't worry, I'll know who you are.'

'Good. I'll look forward to it.'

'So will I,' she said. 'Sort of.'

5

BY JUDGEMENT, SINCE HE HAD STUDIOUSLY followed the signs, rather than luck, he had exited from Hammersmith Tube Station's subterranean concourse by exactly the right staircase. Thus he found himself at the head of King Street. He had judged the time nicely too. It had just gone twenty past seven. He set off westwards as instructed.

It was a fine, even perfect, summer's evening; the air was warm and easy on the skin but a light breeze was keeping at bay any sense of humidity. He found that the slight, elementary act of walking pleased him. However superficially, it gave him a sense of purpose. Otherwise, earlier, he had spent a right bummer of a day.

In the morning he had once more forced himself to go one-on-one with the self-portrait as, central to his sprawl of a room there on its easel, it had nagged at him to come to a completion, a decision. Yes, it was competent ... but, no ... something was lacking. It resembled him down to the last wart, yes, but as a character study it could have been almost anyone ...maybe if instead of goosing the background he were to invent a foreground. Have him staring out from behind bars, for instance. That might explain and take the curse off the wooden expression but no – a gimmick was a gimmick was a gimmick and no more wherever it was deployed ...hmmm ... In the end he had yet again chickened out. Promising himself he could come back to it in a couple of days he had put the dilemma on the back burner. Kidding himself that he was still using his time profitably he had phoned Bearstow's and Thompson's. He had let both firms know that if they were in need of extra drivers he was sitting on the sub's bench and, once more willing to haul his arse on their respective behalves in freelance circulation.

Then, it still not noon, he had done the washing up and had a heavy duty clear-up of the flat. In the afternoon - it had to be done some time anyway, so why not now! – he had gone off to Lidl for a major shop. The hunt for reduced price stickers was one way of breaking up the tedium ...still only three o'clock, though, dammit!

At long last, having put on his good navy blue shirt, his only formal jacket, no tie, of course, he could finally allow himself to lock the flat's own front and then the house's communal street doors behind him and catch a bus to North Greenwich. So eventually to Hammersmith. He kept on down King Street and past the Lyric Theatre across the road. A steady stream of people was flowing along the opposite pavement towards the theatre's entrance and the chatter, the sheer numbers, leant more excitement to the evening. For a moment as he walked on he was tempted to duck into the Two Brewers for a swift half. He resisted the temptation. What was this evening going to cost him? It was a long time since he'd been out on anything resembling a date. Besides, he should try to keep all his wits about him. Now he was passing a series of routine, suburban, closed for the evening shops. There was a take-away and then a restaurant – not, however, the one he was looking for.

Ah! There. That had to be it. Just at the point where King Street stopped being one-way and eastbound traffic had to make a left turn brightness was spilling out into the soft twilight from a generous ground floor window. Yes, La Bella Vista, painted neatly on the main window pane. He pushed the single-leafed glass door open upon a buzz of conversation. The place was over half full: a good sign, that, considering the still fairly early hour. He smelled good smells and realised that he was truly hungry. Moreover he also liked what he saw.

He had been spared the tenth-rate frescoes of Venice or the Colosseum nor did giant, blow-up photos seek to divert attention from the cuisine. Instead, the walls of the quite long dining area before him were painted a discreet shade of old gold that give warmth to the interior they discreetly enclosed. Nor were the tables, set in combinations of rectangular fours and twos, covered in your Godfather red and white chequered tablecloths. The napery was plain white – another modest background to the business of serving food.

He scanned the room. Towards the rear a lone woman, a woman young rather than old, who sat at a table for two, was staring at him fixedly. Plainly Virginia Faulkner. The smudge in his memory began to take on definition. Yes. That was her. He anticipated a waiter who threatened to come and greet him and made his way directly over to her.

Except that she was darker and had an olive toned skin, she was, now he looked at her closely, very like her dead sister. She had the identical basic features, the same bone structure. He could make this comparison from his personal close-up of the sister's last living moments as featured in his recurrent nightmares.

'Ethan Shaw,' he said.

'So I thought,' she said. She had not stood up. 'You're dead on time. It was good of you to come all this way. No trouble getting here, I trust.'

'No problem,' he said and at once felt embarrassed and annoyed that because it was a literal truth he had come out right at the start of things with such a plebian cliché. At this proper glance she seemed well worth not responding to on automatic pilot.

She was the further side of pretty. Beautiful, indeed. She wore her hair, as close to black as made no difference, down as far as her neck and full about her ears. Straight but curled over her forehead it made the perfect setting for her eyes which were a startlingly light blue. Lapiz lazuli, no less. Her nose was long and straight, delicate and strong at one and the same time. It sat above a mouth, its lips neither fat nor thin, that was stretched across a pert thrust of pointed jaw in somehow perfect proportion. She was wearing a simple linen dress of a rich dark blue and at her throat a silvery band somewhere between a necklace and a choker. They were the perfect colours to set off those eyes and the dark hair framing the face. It was a face Van Dyck would have been able to paint with no recourse to his usual anticipation of the flatterer's airbrush. It was a face he would like to portray himself. Her left hand, he had already clocked, displayed neither wedding nor engagement ring.

'What should I call you?' he said sitting down. 'Not Ms Faulkner, I hope.'

'My birth certificate reads Virginia Tryphena Faulkner,' she said. 'But, if you feel obliged to use a vocative, Ginny will do. It's what I usually answer to.'

'Right,' he said. And this time had wits about him enough not to play it straight back.

'So,' she said, 'have you come to tell me stuff or ask me stuff?'

'Both,' he said. But the waiter was at their elbows with large single-sheet menus.

'Something to drink?' the waiter asked. He was certainly Italian but not of the television serial variety. Ethan Shaw looked at Virginia Faulkner.

'Oh, I think we'll go straight to the wine,' she said and looked across the table. 'What do you fancy for your mains?' she said.

'I would point out that tonight's specials,' said the waiter, 'down the bottom there, you see we have pork chops with sage and bream with cous cous.'

'Looks very tempting,' Ginny, then, said. 'But I'll go for my usual sea food risotto, Giorgio.'

'Very good – and for you sir?'

'The fegato, please.'

'Very good,' Giorgio said as if genuinely approving the choice. 'And how would you like it, sir?'

'Thinly sliced, please. And crisp.'

'Crisp, yes. Very good, sir.' Giorgio had made a note.

'So, to drink?'

'I don't mind white,' Ethan Shaw said, 'if you're having sea food.'

'You sure?'

'What's your house white, Giorgio?' Ethan Shaw said.

'Pinot Grigio, sir. Quite gutsy. Etna you know. Good with liver.'

'Sounds fine. We'll go for that, yes.'

He looked the question across the table. She nodded.

'And for starters,' Giorgio said.

'Just bruschetta for me,' Virginia, no, Ginny said.

'And for me too.'

'Very good.'

Giorgio swiftly reclaimed the menus and had disappeared.

'I was tempted by the bream,' Ethan Shaw said but I like liver and I can never get it right at home.'

She looked at him a longish moment.

'You live alone then, do you?' she said.

Well, he didn't wear a ring either. He nodded.

'As it happens,' he said.

'I know nothing about you,' she went on. 'Perhaps we'd better start getting down to basics. What do you do?'

'I'm a student,' he said. And saw her puzzled reaction.

'A pretty old one,' she said.

'Mature is the preferred word, if you don't mind,' he said. 'An Art student. OK, here's me in a nutshell. I'm 29. I was born in

Peckham. I never knew my mother because when I was still a toddler she ran off with one of her fancy men. My father brought me up. He owned and operated a small skip hire company. He taught me to drive when I was 13. As soon as it was legal I got a license and then – I think money may have changed hands – he fixed me up with an HGV license. I was to go into the skip business, you see. I didn't want to. I wanted to stay on at my Comprehensive, you see. There was this brilliant art master there and he'd shown me how to draw and paint. I knew I was good and I enjoyed it but my dad wasn't having any of that old arty-farty malarkey. He wanted my cut-price labour and I was still too young to stand up to him. Besides, I felt sorry for him. So for about a year I carted skips around South East London. King of the road. Then dad made things easy for me. After my mother ran out on him he'd always been a drinker – now, aged 60, he dropped down dead. I was a free man. Only, I'd inherited a business with umpteen debts and some big metal boxes and a ruddy great truck.

'What to do? I sold the business, so called, to the competition down the road and for want of a better idea joined the Army. Something to do, you see.'

'You became a squaddy?'

'Yes.'

'What sort?'

'After I'd suffered the basic training, the Army for once, got it right. I ended up in the Service Corps driving clapped out old Bedfords across Salisbury Plain and, later, in Northern Ireland.'

'That sounds dangerous.'

'No. Boring. Things over there had largely cooled down and in any case I was mainly marooned in barracks inside a military airfield. I divided the time climbing the walls and unpacking big Sikorsky choppers. But also, all the time, I was sketching, drawing.'

'How long were you in?'

'Seven years. When I came out I went back to working for

haulage contractors. I managed to squeeze in some art lessons in evening classes. In the end another ace teacher talked me into applying for a place at his old Art College.'

'Which was?'

'Goldsmith's.'

He saw her eyebrows rise up in surprise.

'Goldsmith's! Impressive. It's pretty up market isn't it?'

'Yes. Me and Frank Keating, God bless his soul. I didn't think I had an earthly of getting in. But I put together a portfolio and my teacher swore on a stack of bibles I was the most promising student he'd ever been lucky enough to meet with – which might also have been true. Anyway they took me. I was so lucky. I learned later that they'd tagged me a 'late bloomer' which made me feel like a loaf of bread.'

'But scarcely half-baked, I take it,' she said.

Giorgio was back. He carried an ice bucket on some kind of tripod. Without flourish he produced a wine bottle and displayed it. Ethan Shaw touched the bottle – good and cold.

'Fine,' he said.

Giorgio nodded his approval of the investigation, uncorked the bottle in a quick clean flash and was stretching forward again.

'Just go ahead and pour, please,' Ethan Shaw said.

Giorgio smiled, serving his female client first, he poured two generous glasses. Then, somehow, he had gone away again.

'Cheers,' Ethan Shaw said and drank. Well, it had alcohol in it.

'Cheers. What medium do you work in?' Virginia Faulkner asked as if there had been no interruption to their dialogue. Polite, good for her, he thought.

'Oil and water colour, mainly.'

'What sort of subjects?'

'I'm very old fashioned. Portraits – that's the oil mainly. And landscapes – that's the watercolour; with lately a small touch of ink line work.'

'No acrylic?'

'I don't like acrylic. Too one dimensional. No depth. So hardly any.'

'What will you hope to do next?'

'God knows. Probably spend my brilliant career knocking out Christmas cards.'

'Where are you in your studies right now?'

'About to go into my third, my last year this coming September. In regard to which it was before I started them – some time before that – when I wasn't quite so lucky. And why we're meeting right now.'

'When Angie drove into you, you mean.'

'Exactly. Look, I'm sorry –'

He found that he had automatically broken off his reply since, as if intent on adding suspense to their evening, Giorgio was back at their table with their bruschetta. Once again he professionally served the lady first.

'Thank you.'

'Buon appetito,' Giorgio murmured and once more had left them.

Hmmm! There had been no need to wish enjoyment on them. Simple as it was, the bruschetta was delicious. Definitely 'more-ish'.

'You were about to say?' she said.

'Oh. Yes. I'm sorry if descending on you like this out of nowhere I've opened up –'

'Hardly from nowhere. And it's not a problem. Not anymore. It was grim, really bloody, but I've come out the other side. I'm living with it. If I say it seems we'll soon be coming to the crunch, the pun will be intentional.'

'Well ...'

'The reason I suggested we meet is a word you brought up on the phone: a simple word beginning with the letter M.'

'Murder.'

'Quite so. Boy, this is really good, isn't it?'

'Delicious.'

'Look, you just showed me yours, let me balance things up. Then you'll know where I'm coming from. I'd say we had a lot in common. We're both loners, dare I say? In a way I'm an orphan too.'

'Oh?'

'Not literarily. You've heard of Faulkner Foundries?'

'Vaguely.'

'My father's companies. Years ago he was a bit of a scientific whizz kid. He devised a way of tweaking the Bessemer process. He developed a way of producing a very tough steel. It earned him millions. Literally. To this day every time our liberal and democratic government slip the Saudis the latest state of the art in the way of armaments my father's process is underwriting the deal.'

'Wow!'

'Double wow in fact. About ten years ago father sold the whole operation to the Arabs. He made a packet; they had themselves a win-win situation on all future deals.'

'So?'

'About this time I was about sixteen. I had finally found out why we were so rich. Ha! Sixteen! Time to rebel. I told my father he was a loathsome man. He was nothing but an arms dealer putting the world at risk. Not a good career move. Mine I mean. He cut me out of his will. Just in time. From his point of view. Three months or so later he dropped dead too.'

'Where did the money go?'

'My sister copped loads.'

'Ouch!'

'At the time I didn't mind. Basically I still don't. Honestly. You see –'

She had broken off. Giorgio was back. Deftly he removed their empty plates. To his chagrin Ethan Shaw clocked that after the first couple of pleasurable bites he had consumed the rest of his bruschetta without tasting it. Damn! he thought as Giorgio turned and left.

'Yes?' he prompted.

'I was a late child,' Virginia aka Ginny said. 'After I was born my mother hated me. Little by little I found out why.'

'Why was it then?'

'My parents loathed each other. Very early on in the marriage they went to separate bedrooms. My father had other women. At first, of course, I had no idea.'

'They didn't divorce?'

'Oh no! Not worth their financial while you see. Nor their *nouvelle riche* social standing. Birmingham bourgeois big-wigs and all that. But one day my father came back from some function ... well, pissed. And horny. He as good as raped my mother. The end result was little accidental me.'

'Who told you this?'

'My sister. I'll come back to this.'

'No abortion obviously.'

'No way. Their sort of people no more countenanced abortion than divorce. You stayed shtum and kept the annual dividends. My mother carried me to term and afterwards at last had something in common with my father.'

'They both detested you.'

'You've got it in one. They both couldn't take being reminded of that 'accident'.'

'It was Angie, my sister, who saved me. She was 12 years older than I, you see. By the time I was old enough to take things in she was another grown-up to me. She was my playmate, my teacher, did my homework with me, took me to galleries, concerts, the cinema. She devoted huge wads of her time to me. She was my real, my spiritual parent.'

She looked up.

'So that's where I'm coming from,' she said.

'Ah...'

Giorgio was back with their main courses. Her risotto looked heavy on the sea food and he could see at one glance that his liver was indeed sliced thin and crisp. It had been a long time since he'd eaten food of this quality. This time he would savour everything down to the last bite.

'You see,' Ginny resumed when they were once more à deux, 'I too have wondered whether the M word might be applicable in this case. So, back in your court. What light do you shine into dirty corners?'

'Quite a lot, I think. A basic one anyway.'

'Namely?'

Bad timing. The liver was terrific. But first things first: he must concentrate on his words now rather than his taste buds. Briefly, he summarised his exchanges with Ayers, Mitchell and Reynolds. He tried to convey the unreal yet, at the same time, peculiarly natural, everyday feel of the incident – the non-incident – in the meadow.

'Well,' she said at long last. 'If what seems obvious is what did happen it was a big mistake of theirs not to plant that key bolt a mile or two back up the approach road where the search would be sure to take place.'

Bright girl.

'I've thought that,' Ethan Shaw said. 'Dead obvious, surely. Seriously stupid not to do that.'

'They are stupid, I reckon,' she said. 'And there is a reason for that, I believe. The same reason that had you being trotted after by a man with a shotgun.'

'So what would that be?'

'If Angie was deliberately murdered what would you say their motive – *his* motive must be?'

' ... bad marriage. And from what you've just told me: money. With an accidental death verdict he must have copped a packet.'

'He did, the bastard. Before the crash despite all his flash – because of all his flash - his nibs was completely down on his uppers. Birchfield Hall was mortgaged up to the hilt. He was haemorrhaging money. But now, of course, he was in clover – debts all wiped clean off the slate. And enough readies in their brown envelopes now to run serious campaigns, come the next election, in the half dozen constituencies where the Independent Nationalists are not completely dead in the water. So, yes, page one is Money.'

Halfway through her risotto she put down her fork and looked searchingly at Ethan Shaw.

'Do you think you'll want a dessert?' she said.

'If it's as good as this.'

'It would be,' she said.. 'But there's more I have to tell – and show. You. Heavy stuff. The coffee's very good here too, but it's no better than the coffee I make five minutes away around the corner. We could talk more freely and openly at mine. It would be more relaxed.'

There was being relaxed, he thought and being so relaxed you're nothing but expectant.

'Let's do yours then,' he said.

6

'WELL,' ETHAN SHAW HAD SAID, 'WE'VE met, we've had dinner together for well over an hour and I still have no idea what, if anything, you do for a nine to five.'

'Nothing spectacular. I work in fashion design.'

'Oh? Like, er Chanel or Worth or ... Balenciaga?'

'Not yet,' Virginia Faulkner had answered.

He had laughed. They were walking back along King Street. While they had eaten dusk had come down and it would soon be dark: but the air, if anything, was even warmer. It seemed to him to have the quality of the soft red wine he would have preferred to go with his liver had he not given cavalier best to her sea food. There were cars enough still coming and going now but very few pedestrians. Obscurely he was glad. When on their getting up to leave the Bella Vista she had stood erect he had instantly perceived that her figure was as sensational as her features. As instantly and inevitably he had hoped that one day it might be literally sensational. But now he was almost embarrassed to have had that so very obvious impulse. He was glad now that there were no casual third-party observers to see them and draw the same over-obvious conclusion: what a couple, made for each other, lucky dog; no question where those two are heading off to!

'Actually,' she was responding, 'I work for a company you've never heard of. Two very English names who design outfits for upmarket, upper middle class outfits like John Lewis and Marks and Spencer. 'Own label lines.' You know, well made, sensible, stylish up to a point without being over the top. Trick is not to be too fancy.'

'You don't seem that enthusiastic.'

'Clearly not. It's hardly that creative. We do the designs and make suggestions about materials – the fabric – and off goes a toile design template, so to speak, to Bangladesh and points East where it can be mass-produced for a fraction of what it would cost here. Then they whip it back to us minus a zipper or a couple of sequins or whatever. We finish it off and that legally allows us to put a 'Made in the UK' label on the item.'

'How do you get to be doing this?'

'Oh, all part of my teenage revolt. I swept out of my disinherited home and got myself a place at St Martin's.'

'St Martin's! That's impressive too.'

'Yes. Good instructors. Like you I was good at Art. Starred A and all that jazz. Unlike you I was allowed to finish my sixth form years. This is me.'

She had lead him away from King Street into the warren of tightly packed two-storey, terraced houses. Post World War One by the look of them. It was a tidy, prettily gentrified area. Audis, BMWs and Mercedes lined the kerbs to left and right. She opened a wrought iron gate.

'Let me lead you up the garden path,' she said.

He had had the same thought.

'You've used that line before,' he said.

She gave him a Mona Lisa look.

'True,' she simply said.

She produced a key to a sophisticated Yale plus lock and swung open the front door.

'After you,' he said. 'You know the way.'

He followed her down a short hallway and on via a door to the left into a longish ground floor room; obviously a knocked-through job he saw at once.

'Just sling your jacket on that sofa,' she said. 'I'll give the coffee its starter for ten.'

'I'm simple,' he said. 'Black and without.'

She left the room via a further side door and him to look around. It was worth doing. The room was tasteful in a way that didn't invite inverted commas. It was quiet and thoughtful. Restful. A deep armchair covered in a mid-greyish fabric was placed towards the room's front window. Its mirror image companion confronted it from the room's rear. A matching two seater sofa stood at right angles to the second chair, a Scandinavian corner table linking them. A sheet of plate glass lay supported on two sandstone blocks to form a coffee table in front of the sofa. Rich velvet or velour drapes rather than curtains were drawn across the front and rear windows to exclude the night-time world. They were a dove grey but he guessed that in daylight and opened they would lighten to almost lilac. What had immediately caught his eye was that on the wall that did not open on to the hall and the kitchen an expensively framed, appropriately large reproduction of Piero's tough kid, street-wise Pregnant Madonna was hung satisfyingly off dead centre. Ah ... There was technique to put you off your own stroke. With restraint he sat down in the rear armchair. The kitchen door swung open again.

'Coming up in the next bucket,' the object of his nascent lust said. She went straight to the sofa and sat down.

'Very nice,' he said, looking around. 'All yours?'

'Lock, stock and all the two and half bedrooms,' Ginny said.

'Wow!'

'Yes, wow. I just got on the ladder in time.'

'How–'

'Despite being cut off without, etcetera, I did have a bit put by.

But the down payment for this all came from Angie. I told you we were close.'

'Lord Snooty didn't mind?'

'I'm sure he did. He's a Lord Scrooge at heart. But there wasn't anything at the time he could do about it and he knew it.'

She looked at him.

'In case you're still wondering why I brought you here,' she said, 'let's get back to our moutons. OK?'

'Let's,' he said.

'So far, including the not so small fortune he stood to inherit we have a great deal of very persuasive but possibly too obvious circumstantial evidence but, that money apart, not much motive. Right?'

'Right.'

'Here's where I can weigh in with a whole heap of motive.'

'Such as?'

'Angie and I talked on the phone at least once a week. A couple of weeks before 'it' – the crash – she told me she was starting to apply for a divorce.'

'Wouldn't have been the end of his world, would it?'

'It would have been for an MP whose support came almost exclusively from traditional, "right-minded" ...'

She had mimed the quotation marks with her index fingers.

'... God-fearing voters. If not the end of his world, certainly the end of his career.'

'Suppose! Certainly you may suppose! What gender do you think the name of any cited corespondent would have been in his divorce proceedings?'

'You mean ...'

'Of course! My beloved erstwhile brother-in-law was – is – gay!'

'Gay?'

'Incorrigibly. As gay as the proverbial clockwork orange.'

'I'd never picked that up.'

'Well I'd bet this house on half the MPs in Westminster knowing it – plus the denizens of God knows how many unsavoury bed-sits across London.'

'All the same. In this day and age, thank God, it's not a crime, is it? A good half a dozen or more MPs have come out, have they not?'

'But they're not leaders of a mickey mouse party – so called. Think of that tweedy hunting squirearchy that voted the sod in. If they wouldn't like the thought of a divorce how do you think they'd react to a gay divorce?'

'Lovely film.'

'What? His political career, his pathetic party will be knocked sideways into kingdom come.'

'All the same ... Push coming to shove now, it would only be your word against his. And his word –'

'Don't you believe it!'

Her getting abruptly to her feet had driven the interruption home fast. She stood looking belligerently down on him.

'The coffee will be ready,' she said.

'And – the reason I brought you back here – I've got something to show you.' She went out the second door.

So, he mused, Hilary Paget-Bourke was gay. Well, public school, university. Once you knew it, it was so clearly obvious ... The chink of crockery next door brought him back to the quiet, gracious room. In a moment Virginia Faulkner, Ginny to her intimates, had returned carrying a tray that held a steaming percolator, cups, a jug and bowl. And some papers. She put the tray down where else but on the glass coffee table.

'Sugar?'

'No thanks. Just as it comes.'

She gave him coffee in the handsome green and gold cup. He waited until she had poured for herself and taken cream but no sugar. When she sat down he took his first sip.

'Umm!' he said. 'Sorry to sound like a commercial but that's good coffee. Great coffee. You weren't making it up – clearly better than the Bella Vista could have managed.'

'Thanks,' she smiled. 'I was almost regretting having said that. You can never be sure with coffee, can you?'

She was picking up a sheet of paper as she spoke. Now she reached it across to him.

'Read this,' she enjoined him.

'What is it?' he asked.

'A photocopy of a photocopy. Read it.'

It seemed to be a handwritten letter. Short. He looked first at the signature, large, florid and evidently descended from copperplate. As he'd expected it was Paget-Bourke's and now he read:

> Dear Stephikins,
> Of course you may draw upon my purse. In for a penny in for a pound. Why should we stop at fifty? Herewith a nice round hundred.
>
> I'm slightly miffed, I have to tell you, that you felt constrained to forward me your passport as an 'advance security'. What are friends for if not to translate their love into good things for one another? This half-arsed pledge of good-will is nothing compared to our full and mutually arsed affection!
>
> I am back up to London in ten days' time for the next Parliamentary session.
>
> And am counting the days until then.
> Loving you to bits,
> Hilly.

Ethan Shaw sat still a while reading the letter through a second time. It had been dated, he now took in, the best part of four years earlier.

'Well,' he said. 'Game, set and match. In the hands of a halfways competent barrister that's dynamite. He must have been insane to commit that to a letter in his own hand.'

'Exactly. Not just my word against his, at all.'

'No. Er ... forgive me – did your sister know about all this?'

'Not when they married. But she soon started picking up vibrations. He wasn't that golden-haired an Apollo after all. I never pressed her for details but things soon started to go pear-shaped in the bedroom. Essentially he didn't want to know. The tradition of separate bedrooms runs through the Faulkner generations, it would seem.'

'But the two of them did provide you with two nieces.'

'You know what she said to me he said?' she said. 'At one time they had a furious knock-down row and do you know what he said about Imogen and Cordelia?'

'What?'

'That they were window dressing – necessary for the photo opportunities!'

'The bastard!'

'Quite.'

'She did confront him then?'

'Oh yes. Quite early on. He was abject at first. Blamed Eton.'

'Of course.'

'Swore he was devoted to her and he would change his ways but, of course, no. He didn't mean a word of it. The bastard couldn't change his tacky spots. Soon he wasn't even going through the motions.'

'The poor thing.'

'She tried to tough it out. She didn't go looking for solace in some hunky pairs of accommodating arms. But about six months before the crash she'd had enough. She started to talk to me about divorce. She believed she had enough of a case, enough evidence, to gain possession of her daughters.'

'You'd reckon.'

'You know that letter reminds me of what in its way is probably the most shocking thing about the whole case – and the most terrible.'

'Yes?'

'You remember the wreckage was all the more difficult to untangle because the Mini had been full of suitcases and bags?'

'Yes.'

'Well the reason for that that they were all coming to London to get him into position for a new Parliamentary session. They'd taken a lease on a house in Cleaver Square, a little island of Georgian gems just down from Westminster in Kennington. Originally they were all going to motor up in the Range Rover Vogue, bags and all. But the night before she died she phoned me saying that he and the girls were coming by train.'

'As they did, I remember.'

'Yes,' she said. 'He'd persuaded her the Mini would be better in traffic-clogged London, so she was going to bring it up in the morning.'

'She was. Not him.'

'Exactly.'

'What a shit. If that doesn't seal it! Is he still in that posh square?'

'No. That was then. These days he camps out – in every sense no doubt – in Goldolphin Square.'

''Well that covers a multitude of sins right there.'

'Here's still more ammunition. Read this.'

She had handed him a second photocopy. Typewritten this time, it was a second, longer letter. Once more he looked at the concluding signature. It was not a name he recognised. Stephen Saunders.

> Dear Mrs Paget-Bourke,
> If you glance at the name (mine) at the foot of this letter it will almost certainly mean nothing to you. We have not met. It will, however, mean something to your husband who I have met. Some years ago when a young man (I am still – just – in my twenties) I was in contact with him when I was living in his constituency. I was hoping (having made a botch of my Higher Education) to obtain a job in the world of banking and I wrote to him seeking his advice and support. We met then and seemed to get on very well and as well as assuring me of his good offices he ended the meeting by

inviting me to dinner. I gladly accepted this windfall. Subsequently, mainly in London (I had moved there in search of work when the banking position failed to materialise), we met socially on numerous further occasions. Finally, finding myself in a particularly tight financial corner I was so bold as to ask him for a loan. He was kind enough to lend me one hundred pounds (I had asked for fifty!) As a surety (if that is the right word) I forwarded him voluntarily, my idea, my passport. I have long since paid back the money but to-date he has not returned the passport to me. This despite my several requests that he should. Indeed, of late, he seems to be ignoring me.

Not having my passport is a major nuisance for me. Not so long ago I had the chance of employment (a proper job) in the Irish Republic but obviously without my passport I could not cross over to follow the chance up on the spot. Nor can I apply for a new passport, since, I am too financially constrained at present to pay for one at present nor is my original passport genuinely lost.

I would ask, then, to put it mildly, if you could be kind enough to jog your husband's memory on my behalf. I do not think this request is too inordinate even though I am unknown to you because I ask from him no more than what is clearly mine. He has always said to me that you are 'the boss' at home and I therefore believe, perhaps fondly, that a word from you might stick where dozens from me slip right by. Mail addressed to me at the above address will find me for the foreseeable future. Yours sincerely,

Stephen Saunders.

Ethan Shaw placed the letter back down upon the glass table. Ginny Faulkner had not breathed a word, had scarcely breathed at all while he had been reading.

'Well?' she now said.

'Fairly literate,' he said. 'Not completely. A lot of brackets.'

'A sign of insecurity, I imagine. And ...?'

'Put these two letters together – in the originals – and even a totally incompetent brief would get a result.'

'I should bloody well hope so! Don't worry, I've got the originals. Angie sent them both to me.'

'Have you tried doing anything with them?'

'I showed them off-line to a young trainee legal eagle I happen to know socially.'

'What did he say?'

'She wasn't encouraging. She said Hillsborough was a spectacular exception, not a precedent. I'd have minimal chance of getting Angie's inquest verdict turned over after such a long time lapse. And, of course, not being married to him, I can't divorce him, bugger or not. I mean, get him into court that way.'

'No.'

Ethan Shaw sat for a while thinking.

'So how can you be sure I'm not gay,' he said at last.

'Oh I'm pretty much satisfied you're not,' Ginny Faulkner said.

'Based on what?'

'The way you've been looking at me on and off most of the evening.'

'Incontrovertible evidence. What do you propose doing about it?'

'What? You and me?'

'Me and you: you and me ... I mean, even my PTSD disturbed slumbers have got to seem pretty small beer compared with what that stuck-up bugger's been getting away with.'

'Thanks a lot.'

'You know what I mean.'

'Yes. I do.'

She leaned forward. The blue dress suited her so well.

'Look,' she said, 'a few moments ago you were nice enough to compliment me.'

'Yes.'

'Well, I'll have you know that however well I make coffee I make breakfast twice, no, three times, no, ten times better. It's always silly when two loners, as I previously described us, who happen to find themselves in pretty much the same spot don't link up to change their mutual status. Also I've no wish to see the

Faulkner family tradition of separate bedrooms spreading sideways through its members. Consequently for the last half hour I've been toying with the idea of making you breakfast tomorrow.'

'Only ...'

'Only: with Angie in my head so much tonight and our having met caused by such a black moment, to dance the light fantastic here and now would seem ... would seem really ...'

'Tacky: to use one of your words.'

'Yes.'

'Yes, it would.'

'And the main event?'

'Albeit in bedrooms separated by the width of London let us both sleep on it. I'll put breakfast on the back burner.'

'Ho ho. OK. Deal.'

As for your nightmares – you know full well you're squeaky clean. Stop having them.'

'It's not that I've ever felt guilty,' he said. 'It was just being there. Seeing it.'

He shouldn't have said that.

'I'll have some more coffee, then I'll go,' he said.

7

KING STREET, WHEN HE ENTERED UPON it for a third time, had changed its character. Dark was no longer dusk and with the waning of the light, chill had fallen from the air. Ethan Shaw was glad of the warming sense of the two cups of rich coffee in the pit of his stomach as he made his way back towards the tube station. Deserted, the street seemed lonely now. Menacing. There were no other pedestrians whatsoever at this in-between hour and the westbound cars swishing by were all blatantly taking advantage of the chance to speed.

When, utterly without incident, he reached the station concourse it seemed an in-between time of night there too. The long platform where he had to wait for a seemingly unduly long time was all but completely lacking in other travellers. Only a group of four or five teenagers at its far end shared his wait and emphasised its duration with their high-pitched echoing babble. When the air at last whooshed clatteringly in from out the tunnel's mouth the arriving carriages were almost all empty. Too early for theatre goers going home, he realised, far too late for office workers commuting back to home. The two ageing women who faced him across the carriage as he sat on the nearest seat to hand had seamed, dog-tired faces and appeared not so much to ignore him but, in their evident fatigue, not to notice him at all. Chars possibly, he thought, office cleaners – but whether on their way in to work right now or on their own way home, well, who could say? Hundreds would have used this carriage in the course of the day, thousands, shift-workers or nine-to-fivers packed like sardines. Well he was well out of that. Not for a Canary Wharf king's ransom would he want to imprison himself in so mindless and soul-less a cul-de-sac.

Hmmm ... Canary Wharf ... Still miles away. His own homewards bound journey seemed to be taking three times as long as the outward. Probably due to the sense of surrounding, played out emptiness. He should improve the unshining hour by putting his mind to work. God knew after tonight he'd picked up more than enough to try and think through into order. Only ... just this minute he didn't want to. He'd just lucked into stumbling upon a 22-carat diamond lady who had broadcast unequivocally that she fancied him. How many light years had passed since that had happened? Yes, a mind like that, a figure like that: and she'd asked him if he worked in acrylic? Marriage of two minds,or what? Well, not to rush things ...

At Green Park where he had to change, the two women left the carriage as well. Definitely going in to work then. And leaving him to another subterranean route march, another almost interminable wait on an almost deserted platform until, at last, what might have been the same train, unfurled more empty seats and occasional wizened faces into decelerating sight.

Only when he came to the third connection in his journey – tube to bus – did his luck change. On emerging from the long trek up to ground level at North Greenwich he caught sight of his bus already halted and taking on board a long line of suddenly materialised passengers at its stop the best part of fifty yards away. Reviving his outside-centre's burst of instant speed he made it to the end of the peristaltic file just in time to beat the thumped behind him clattering-to of the doors. Standing room only. After famine, claustrophobic feast. Panting he stood his ground as the bus jolted off.

A different crowd this. Younger, still hopeful. He just had time to clock the tableau of multi-ethnic faces pretending not to look at him turning into multi-styled scalps almost as if in response to an order. Male, female, it made no difference. In all seats it was eyes down for a session on the smart phone. Where had they all come from? There were a few deadpan and dead-beat older passengers but the majority must have come from table-tennis league games, hot dates that had petered out, trivial pursuit nights in The Dog and Duck. The suburbs bred a different class of loser to the city ...

The bus weaved in and out of sidestreets feeding the bypass. Now he had to brace himself as, to beat the changing lights, it took a roundabout too fast. People were actually using their phones for talk now. At least three different languages were sending messages out into the sodium street-lit night. Bright inside the bus, dark outside. Detached reflections in the windows. Edward Hopper lived.

His turn now to press the 'Stop' button. After the frowsty babble of the bus it felt good to find himself completely alone again and walking through the clean, cold darkness. Ginny Faulkner, eh. There was a lady to take your hat off to. And whatever else – to forget all that for the moment – he had her number. He knew where she lived.

He turned the last corner and fished out his keys. For a second he thought he had mixed them up. The lock to 34's street door resisted his usual turn then, however, as he tried again, it yielded. He went into the miniscule lobby area and had no problem at all unlocking the second door opening on to the staircase. Not wanting to disturb the other tenants he went quietly up the stairs in total darkness, something he had long since grown used to, and emerged on to the first floor landing. There was a glimmer of light from outside. Here too there was a hint of something different, a vibration nothing more, that brought him up short. He switched on the landing light. The door to his own apartment stood ajar. It was more than half open.

He swallowed. He knew for a certain fact that he had locked the door behind him on leaving. That was page one in a place like this. Now ... He moved forward and examined the Yale lock and the door jamb. Both were completely intact. Neither gave witness to a false entry. Perhaps, distracted in an anticipation of his evening he had forgotten to lock up after all. No he hadn't. He stepped through the doorway into his room and nobody zapped him with a black-jack. He braced himself and eyes darting from side to side, switched on the main overhead light.

Nothing. Nobody. At first glance everything was where it should have been and nothing was missing. Everything was as it should be and just as he had left it.

And yet it wasn't. An eerie difference hung chillingly in the air. Somebody had been here in his absence. Not moving, slowly and carefully now, he once more scanned the room. No, nothing – not that there was much to take – had gone. Paints, brushes, jars were all in place. The prehistoric television still held its corner, the rail he used in lieu of a wardrobe still carried the miserable full complement of his clothes. What then? What?

A car went by outside. Towards the window, diagonally across from him, his own portrait of himself as a fairly young artist regarded him derisively through the wan inadequate light. Mysteriously, it had come on while he'd been away, had matured. It was better than he'd remembered. He moved toward it to see why this should be. Then in mid-stride he froze. He could see now and seeing gave him instant and seriously frightened pause.

The features in the portrait – it be-all and end-all – were now plumper and more diffuse. For a simple reason. Someone had taken a blade and made a series of vertical cuts in the canvas running straight down from the forehead to the thick neck. They were fine cuts: the face was in strips not tatters. The intruder must have used a razor. Old-fashioned but eternally effective. And he got the new picture. An icy coldness divided itself between the back of his throat, the pit of his stomach and his scrotum. His knees went weak. This was a message, a clear warning – and, no two ways about it, he felt warned. Now his nostrils were adding to his alarm. Belatedly he had become aware that the pungent turpentiny smell which was part and parcel of working in oils and which he was so accustomed to that he never noticed it was no longer thickening the air. He had not put brush to canvas in days. The rich smell had been reduced to a thin, sourish, lingering odour. It did not bode well. It was not the sweet smell of success. Faintly lavatorial it smelt the way the painting looked and how he felt. Reboot time. He sat down on the room's solitary armchair to think things through.

He had heard people who'd been burgled saying that it was like suffering a lesser version of rape and now he knew for himself that this was true. Tip though it was, this room had been violated and that was why he was trembling. Strangers had been here. For the moment the warning element was irrelevant. This room had been where his life had brought him. Not so much of a life, maybe: But it hadn't deserved to be spat upon.

He took deep breaths. Think! Think! In a while he could and his trembling stopped.

The intruder, for a start, had rendered him one huge incidental favour. There was no longer any need to keep shilly-shallying in his mind over whether he could afford to pretend to himself that the self portrait did a job. The truth was it never quite had and, now that it was obviously a write-off as a course project, he had no option but to start over from scratch. But this defaced – ha! – oil version did now suggest how he should shift gear – looser, more blurred, yes, plumper. Water colour therefore and, excuse the pun, an attempt at a two-faced, multi-face impression. Good. He'd had his mind made up for him. Meanwhile ... The warning hadn't been irrelevant.

He looked around the room. His bed was tucked away in the further corner but how could he sleep soundly in it now? The room was as pregnable as a shoe-box. When Mrs Henderson had her buy-to-let house converted into flats they had done no more for his apartment than to bung a Yale lock on the already existing interior door of the original main bedroom. The door and its frame were barely more than matchwood. A swift kick from any heavy older than eight years would grant entrance at four o'clock of any cold and frosty morning. Kipping here, he had to concede you were no more than a sitting duck.

Hmmm ... He had been away. What would they have done if he'd been in? No, don't go there. Think positive. All right, he had come back. He'd put on the light. Probably they – someone – had been outside waiting and watching. They would have clocked him returning. They could be outside right now. OK, fight fire with fire.

He got out of the chair and switched off the overhead light. He walked to the window and drew the curtain closed, then fetched out his phone. It was not in his case to call Eritrea from a suburban London bus.

'Which service?' a voice asked.

'Police,' he replied.

If you could regard a lapse of just short of fifty minutes as rapid, the police response to his emergency call might be regarded as rapid. Ethan Shaw could be precise about the length of the delay because he had spent the pregnant interval between call and arrival alternating glances at his watch with clocking the street outside and below through the slit left by the minimal curtain to the side of his now darkened room's front window. The wait at least allowed his breathing and pulse to stay put at a rate he might consider normal. During it he did not see a single pedestrian go by the house. Three cars came and went but none of them suggested for a moment that they were anything other than casual bypassers. On the other hand when a fourth pair of headlights swung round the corner he knew somehow at once that his red alert vigil was over.

The car drew to a halt where there was a parking spot a few doors down the street. Although a Peugot it bore the conventional jam-sandwich livery of a British police car. To his disappointment when the two men inside got out they were both wearing uniforms. The one held a piece of paper and both were looking between what it told them and the fronting row of house fronts.

He would still do his best to preserve his fellow tenants' beauty sleep. He stepped quickly across his room and this time switching on the light in the well went down the stairs. When he opened the house's front door on to the outside world he received a shock. The one policeman, frozen in the mid-action of reaching for the squawk box bell, the two of them stood there as startled and slack-jawed as he must have seemed to them.

'Christ!' the one to the rear exclaimed. 'You take some chances!'

'I do?'

'... Mr Shaw?'

'Yes.'

'You reported a forced entry, yes?'

'Yes. Upstairs. On the first floor. My flat. I'll show you.'

He lead the way upstairs and knew from the heavy, arhythmic thudding of the clumping behind that his concern for his neighbours' sound slumbers had been beside the point. On the tiny, vestigial landing outside the again open door to his room he halted.

'I was out this evening,' he said. 'I got back here about a quarter to eleven. I had a bit of trouble opening the front door down there and when I got upstairs this one was ajar. Open. I know for certain I'd locked it when I went out.

'What time was that?'

'About 6.30.'

The two coppers were looking at the door's lock and its frame.

'Hasn't been forced,' one said. 'Woodwork's still in one piece.'

'You could open this with a putty knife,' the other said dismissively. 'No alarm or CCTV, I suppose?'

'No.'

'Pity. What's been taken then?'

'Nothing I can see so far.'

'Let's have a butcher's then.'

Switching on its main light, he led them into the room-cum studio. They stood just inside the threshold their faces slack with a bewilderment that rapidly hardened into contempt.

'Hardly anything in here worth nicking,' the faintly shorter one said, 'is there?'

'True. But even so –'

He took a first good look at them. They were probably near as to being twins as two unrelated individuals could possibly be. That was partly the uniforms, of course, but their resembling each other ran much deeper. Both were about five nine, both chunky. Both had too much flesh about their cheeks and throat. Both had, not shaven heads, but hair cropped so short across their scalps it must have required treatment every other day. Both had eyes with that washed-out grey colour so quick to register cynicism, suspicion and disdain. Neither had been civil enough to introduce themselves but they both bore an identification of sorts in the numbers spelled out in metallic digits on their chests, 361 and 417. Fleetingly the thought flashed across Ethan Shaw's mind that back at their station there might be an Identikit image of what the ideal copper was officially supposed to look like and that everyone on the force should mimic this ideal. But no, a manual of on the job 'dos and donts' would be as much as it would run to. Their similarity would stem from their belonging to a pack and its collective conforming to a copycat trend. So it was with the rank and file of all large scale institutions – merchant banks, universities, Parliament. Conform and you were exclusive. This pair of bookends felt safer exerting their petty authority as clones.

Early thirties Tweedledum and Tweedledee. No guns but batons on their belts. Hard-boiled – or so they would like to believe themselves.

'I mean,' 417 was saying, 'how old's that tele over there?'

'No idea. I can't get Freeview on it.'

'Nothing taken, you reckon?'

'I don't think so.'

'How'd you know you didn't go out and leave the door open and come home half pissed and put two and two together to make five? I mean, being fair, it's such a tip in here, no-one would consider turning it over.'

'One: because at no time tonight have I been pissed. Two: because I'm a grown-up. Three: I have an excellent memory. Four: because while I've not had anything taken, whoever broke in has caused damage.'

'Like what?'

'Like this.'

Ethan Shaw walked over to his easel and running his fingers down the back of his self portrait made its features ripple.

'They slashed this canvas down the middle with a blade,' he said.

Curious for the first time the two policemen walked towards the painting and deigned to consider it.

'That's not bad that is,' 361 said. 'D'you do it?'

'Yes.'

'Very life-like. Very real. Is it insured?'

'It's not worth anything, so you needn't bother to go there.'

'What are you, then?'

'An art student.'

'Oh, I see. Living in luxury on a grant, are we?'

'You've just pointed out I live in a tip.'

'No call to get sarky.'

'So why would anyone cut up your painting for you?' 417 came quickly in with.

'No idea,' Ethan Shaw lied. Dealing with these churls was not going to get him anywhere. 'Probably frustration at, as you've kindly pointed out, not finding any rich pickings.'

'Yeah – possible,' 417 nodded. 'Bloody mindedness.'

'Anyone that you know of got it in for you?' 361 redundantly insisted.

'No-one I know of,' Ethan Shaw lied again. 'I'm way too under the radar to make enemies.'

361 and 417 looked at each other and without moving further muscles mutually shook their heads.

'Well,' 361 said, 'that's about it, then, isn't it? Nothing much more we can do here.'

The tone of finality in his voice did not quite disguise the underlying glee.

'Excuse me!'

'Well nothing taken, you say. No reports of breaking and entering from any other occupants of the building ...'

'No point in doing a trawl of pawn and junk shops for items that are still here,' 417 chimed in with.

'What about fingerprints?'

'Won't be any will there,' 361 said. 'We could send somebody along but ...'

'Bloody hell!'

'Oh don't worry. It'll be a statistic. We'll log it, bring it up at tomorrow's roster. We'll give you a case number for the insurance.'

'You're joking. I don't want a case number. I don't want a statistic – I want action. I don't want a somebody! I want a grown-up.'

'Watch it sonny!' 417 barked.

'Don't you sonny me!' Ethan Shaw barked back. 'I'm near as dammit as old as you two. I've got a seven year stretch as a regular soldier under my belt. Finished up a corporal. Believe me I've got just as much experience as you at wriggle-worming out of forms filling in for the sake of filling in forms..'

361 and 417's shoulders both went back as they mirrored each other's aggrieved and affronted but nevertheless troubled look.

'Temper, temper,' 361 sneered.

'You're the one's should watch it,' Ethan Shaw said. 'You haven't been sufficiently arsed enough to give me any names yet but I've got your numbers – literally – and if I don't get to see a grown-up early – I'll be straight on the blower to your nick. And I'll write a letter of complaint. To your Super or whomever. You'll end up with enough paperwork to keep you indoors at your desks for days!'

The features of the two positively recoiled and then tried to make a joint stand.

'Not heard of threatening behaviour, it seems,' 417 said. 'Who does she think she is?'

Rattled, 361 appeared not to know.

'Pongs in here as well,' he managed.

'A member of the public you're supposed to protect and serve,' Ethan Shaw supplied. 'Now fuck off out of here and leave me to work out how I'm going to get some sleep tonight.'

He took a sharp step forward and balefully, as unceremoniously as synchronised swimmers they went. He stared no less balefully at the open doorway which suddenly seemed to gape wider open than the entrance to the channel tunnel. What? How?

It hadn't been an idle question. He'd needs to get old-fashioned bolts for the door; perhaps if he folded his easel flat, wedged it under the handle, braced it with the armchair he could make a temporary barricade that would last long enough, cause enough noise, to have him out of bed and on his feet by the time Chummy came back with his baseball bat. Or ... he could spend the night in the armchair ... drag his bed across the door ...

He heard the Peugot start up outside. Tossers! He didn't feel the least like sleeping anyway.

In the end he had settled for the easel solution. It might buy him some precious few seconds. He had gone to bed with the hammer and kitchen knife he used for stretching and framing and such strategically to hand. But it had, of course, been a terrible night. It had been like sleeping on a drum. Every creaking relaxation of the house's woodwork, each occasional footfall outside had him zooming back up from semi-consciousness to full red alert. For minutes after, only too well aware of every passing minute he lay, eyes closed but stretched and tense. When, starting up yet again to find a begrudging light creeping into the room and his watch saying 6.15 he abandoned his last hope of golden slumbers. Getting up he made coffee and then toast. The good news was that he was still unbloodied and in one piece: absolutely nothing further untoward had happened. Nor had his recurring nightmare recurred.

He was sitting staring at the slashed portrait now propped again the wall when, making him jump, the room's never used intercom croaked into rusty life.

'Arrch ... Mr Shaw?'

'Yes. Hello?'

'Detective Inspector Bradley, Metropolitan Police.'

'Oh, right. Fine. I'll be right down.'

Venturing into the flat-letting game Mrs Henderson had run to the intercom but not to any remote locking system. Already in jeans and t-shirt he went down the stairs and opened the street door. Confronting him on the step was a man of average height and a puzzlingly remarkable complete ordinariness.

He seemed the further end of middle age and was wearing a suit which indicated that it had once been in a Prince of Wales check with a hint of lilac woven into its rectangular pattern. Now, although it seemed clean enough, it had faded, its vertical and horizontal lines merging into a universal dun colour, emphasising that it was shiny and frayed at lapel edge and cuffs. As worn was the tie, its design the diagonal stripe of some unrecognisable school, club or regiment, which conveyed the same shabbiness. The face above was a match. Neither round nor long it hinted at having been of a fair complexion before age and long suffering had reduced it to this grey coarse wan shade. Two cobwebs of fine wrinkles surrounded both lustreless brown eyes and deep lines ran obliquely downwards from the nostril wings into a pincer movement on the mouth. Hair neither fair in colour, brown or grey, screwed out from the point high on the scalp where its front line had receded from the furrowed forehead. It was the tired face of a man stuck with a life-long, hard paper round.

Ethan Shaw had been able to note the shine on the cuff, the loose threads, because Bradley from the first had been patiently holding up in plain sight a cheap plastic wallet which displayed his police identity card. He hadn't assumed a mastery of speed reading on the observer's part but held it open and still. A bled-out photograph of perhaps fifteen years earlier showed the same face sharper and topped by a full head of springy hair. Perhaps the features had once conveyed hope as well as resemblance to those Bradley, indeed - his first name was Alec – had shown the likeness.

'Ah,' said Ethan Shaw, 'the early bird catches the worm.'

'About the break-in last night,' Bradley said at last dropping the ID card out of sight.

'Right. Good. Come on up.'

They went up the stairs. On the threshold of the first floor room Bradley paused. He looked searchingly at the frame and the door lock. He pushed the tongue of the lock in and out twice and then, conspicuously, as he stepped into the room, said nothing. He looked round at the duly revealed studio.

'Spartan,' he said.

'But I call it home,' Ethan Shaw said. 'Or did.'

Bradley smiled in a heard-it-all before way.

'Well, you ruffled a few feathers last night,' he said.

'Not unintentionally. Want a coffee? There's some just made.'

'Yes please,' Bradley said, 'I'd love a cup. I need more and more kick-starting these days. Just black, please. No milk or sugar.'

He had a thin estuary English voice as tired as the rest of him.

'Thank you very much,' he said, taking the proffered mug and drinking. 'Ah, wonderful. Real coffee.'

Tired, maybe, but at least he had manners.

'Why intentionally then?' he asked

'I didn't like them, those two. I didn't trust them. They never gave me their names. I never got past their numbers.'

'Metcalfe and Price, as it happens.'

'A plod by any other name is still a plod.'

'That's hardly complimentary.'

'Again, by intent. I told them I wanted to speak to a grown-up.'

'Well you'll have to make do with me.'

'You'll do.'

'But why? This does all seem pretty trivial.'

'Because I didn't rate them I withheld information from them.'

'Oh?'

'They asked me if I knew of anyone who might have it in for me. I told them I didn't. That wasn't the truth. I do.'

'Oh? Do you possibly feel able to tell me?'

Ethan Shaw let out a long sigh. He indicated the solitary armchair still on back-up duty by the door.

'You'd best sit down,' he said. 'This is going to take a while. You'll see why I didn't want to burden their intelligences with it.'

Bradley moved to the chair, slewed it around to face the room's interior and sat.

'O.K.' he said.

Ethan Shaw sighed again and then starting with the original head-on crash told Bradley of all his private investigations since.

All he omitted was any mention whatsoever of the involvement in the matter of Virginia Faulkner.

Bradley listened without a single interruption. He seemed to grow more still as the account went on. When Ethan Shaw at last fell silent he said a curious thing.

'Well it's a small world and no mistake. A very small world.'

'What do you mean by that?'

'I'll come to that in a second. First, you did well not to reckon Metcalfe and Price. Prime Costa del Sol material between you and me. They wouldn't have wanted to know. Well now, beyond what I've read in the papers I know nothing about your Paget-Bourke. I've heard a couple of pretty seamy rumours but I've heard those sort of rumours about most people. My rule of thumb is to ignore such – it's called innocent till proved guilty. However ...'

'Yes?'

Bradley squirmed in the chair as he pulled a thoughtful face. He got to his feet and began to pace about.

'Now I'm going to make a speech,' he said. 'About it being a small world. If we ever find ourselves in a court of law, I may, I warn you, deny I ever told you a word of about what I'm about to tell you now, but in the meantime ...'

He looked suddenly at Ethan Shaw with a sharpness in his eyes that no longer seemed surprising.

'That ex-copper who conveniently turned up on your doorstep in Sidcup would he by any possible chance answer to the name of Ayers?'

'He would indeed.'

Bradley thumped his right fist excitedly into the palm of his hand. It wasn't just the caffeine getting to him.

'I knew it!' he exclaimed. 'Now, listen. My patch has a lot of des-res property in it. Blackheath, Chislehurst ... We get more than our fair share of breaking and enterings. By and large we know who's responsible and by and large we get them in the end.

But we've got four long standing 'unsolveds' on our list. Three private homes and a jeweller's shop in Orpington - in every case jewels were the main items taken. Very clean efficient thieving. Virtually no clues to follow up on. Four perfect, if you like, crimes spread out over a period of about two years. And with one thing in common. All four premises had security systems installed by Ayers Security.

'Wow!' said Ethan Shaw.

'Nothing we could prove or make stick, mind you. We chatted to him, naturally, and he claimed to have no more idea about it than we did.'

'He would say that wouldn't he?'

'To coin a phrase. Yes. He, of course, pointed out that Ayers Security had installed systems into dozens and dozens of places that had not been turned over. But these four would have been the most lucrative targets to come his way.'

'And when I went and talked to him he boasted of having a locksmith who could open anything and a whiz-kid who could do the same electronically.'

'Exactly. Food for thought, isn't it?'

'No proof?'

'Not a sausage. And there's been no new caper in months. Of course it's not in the interests of his legit business if he goes around busting into every place he's supposed to have made burglar proof. What was the name of the copper Ayers rescued from stage-fright?'

'Reynolds.'

'No. Don't know of him.'

'He was stationed in Cheltenham I think before he quit to go and work for Paget-Bourke.'

'Hmmm. Well I've got a few contacts down in the West Country. I can ask around a bit. Mind you, this theory they nobbled the missus's car. It's a bit crude, isn't it?'

'Yes if that's how it was, it was. It is.'

'Right.' Bradley sniffed. He looked around the room taking it in.

'Coming back to the here and now,' he said. 'I'd reckon that what you told me earlier – that you're sure they broke in not to steal but put the frighteners on you – is absolutely on the money.'

'Well they bloody well succeeded. I was really shaken. I still am. They've made the place seem ... dirty. Not in the way it really is.'

'Quite subtle really. Those razor slashes.'

'Yeah, seeing me there in replica kind of did them a big favour.'

'Not to mention that you're not being here at the time probably did you quite a favour too.'

'Oh?'

'If you had been here you might well have been on the receiving end of quite an unhealthy dose of GBH.'

'It had crossed my mind. It still does. What I don't understand is how the hell they got to know where I live.'

'To coin a phrase. Well, go on Twitter, do you?'

'Certainly not. Nor Facebook either.'

'But you use Amazon. You probably got most of those books over there on AbeBooks.'

'Yes, actually.'

'There you are then. You have accounts like that you are open to the IT world. Certainly to the sort of electronic whiz-kid you say Ayers has got working for him. You've had no secrets from them. You're the one who's the open book in their case.'

'Shit!'

'Yes. Believe me.'

Once more Bradley surveyed the room.

'This is a very flimsy set-up here,' he went on. 'You might do better going into digs somewhere for a couple of weeks.'

'I can't begin to afford that.'

'So perhaps you should take up art forgery.'

'I'm not that good.'

'No friend or relative you can doss down with?'

'No.'

The monosyllable had escaped his lips before the wild hope surged daylight into the back of his mind.

'Well,' he said. 'I might have if I think about it long enough.'

'Be an idea,' Bradley said. He reached into the vest pocket of his less than prepossessing suit as he began to move towards the door and produced a card and after it an IKEA pencil. He wrote something on the back of the card.

'This is me,' he said. 'Anything happens, let me know. What's yours?'

Ethan Shaw told him. Bradley scribbled it down on the back of a second card.

'Let's keep in touch,' he said.

Opening the excuse for a door he paused in the flat's entrance.

'Apologies for Metcalf and Price,' he said.

'They were pure Hillsborough.'

Bradley winced and made no effort to hide that he had.

'No ever apologising for that,' he said. 'Mind you, nobody likes that shift. It brings out the worst in everyone.'

'That's no excuse'

'No. It's not.'

Unexpectedly, awkwardly even, Bradley took a step back into the room.

'Look,' he said. 'Agree to buy a barrel of rotten apples for whatever reason and when you get it home, you'll find they've stuffed you up with two or three perfectly good ones. I've been in the force too long for not enough reward. All the same I've teamed with one mate who bought it going one-on-one against a thug with a gun and another who got crippled down to a desk job by another. Some of us still try.'

'I realise that,' Ethan Shaw said after an embarassed moment. 'Good to have met you.'

He took a step forward so as to shake Bradley's hand.

'OK. Talk later,' Bradley said. 'Don't try to be too clever.'

*

To begin with everything was exactly as it had been the first time. Once again he was in Sidcup in less than ten minutes. Once again he parked in the same side street in possibly the identical spot. The office-cum-shop on the corner still gleamed its darkish blue probity to the world as he approached it this second time. When he pushed through the single-panelled glass front door again, the larger outer office had not altered in any visible way.

Once more nobody sat in the large faux-posh chair at the desk on his right. Once more the large, fleshy Ayers wearing probably the same city-slicker suit was seated in the chair's opposite number behind the left hand desk. Once more he lifted his head up sideways with the beginning of an insincere bright welcome and once again his expression slithered down into wary recognition.

'You,' Ayers said shortly. 'What brings you back?'

'Take a wild guess.'

'No idea,' Ayers said unconvincingly. He couldn't quite hold Ethan Shaw's steady gaze.

'Look,' Ayers contrived, 'I don't have time to play silly –'

'I've come with a message,' Ethan Shaw said. 'A message and a friendly warning. A warning you shouldn't ignore.'

'Like what?'

'The message is: I can take a hint. Pass that on up the line. I'm not looking for grief. I'm going to let well enough alone.'

Ayers ducked his head in a swivelling motion, he seemed to swallow, he did not look to be a happy man.

'I still haven't a clue what you're on about,' he said.

'Well I'm not going to paint you a picture. Understand? The warning relates to that jewellery shop caper in Orpington. Remember?'

'What of it?'

Ayers' right hand was creeping toward his top right drawer.

'You won't need that. I'm out of here this next minute. The local force tell me they know exactly who did it; they just don't have any concrete evidence. Very clever job. Only - quit while you're ahead. Make it the last. Don't just take my word. Have a word with Price and Metcalfe next Lodge meeting, eh?'

Ayers' flabby mouth opened and then, as words failed him, shut. Ethan Shaw, his mission accomplished, turned on his heel and walked out into what he discovered was the sunshine of a warm morning.

He also found as he walked back to his car that he was feeling hot and bothered. He'd supplied Bradley with the hint of a promise that he would let well enough alone. He'd reneged on that immediately. He had to think that meant he remained committed to more positive action on his own account. But should he? And what action? Only fools found it necessary to keep proving that they were their own man. Damn. He got back into the Toyota. The driver's seat creaked and sagged as per usual. Yes, he was a tough guy hero! Fool! He looked at his watch. Still not mid-day. But she would be out of the tube by now in her office or whatever. He took out his mobile and put the last number he'd entered into its cell list into bleeping action.

'Virginia Faulkner.'

The formal BBCish voice. A touch acidic. A suggestion of hostile edge. Yes! In one. He could detect a wash of background activity.

'Hi. Your favourite autodidact here.'

'Yes. Hello. I thought you'd ring. Did ...'

'Listen. No names, no pack-drill. No location. Things have happened down here.'

'Is there a problem?'

The softer voice. Lower in tone.

'Nothing too pressing. Relax. But I need to lie low for a few days; need to bury my head.'

'Pressing is just how that sounds.'

'I can best explain face-to-face. Can you put me up for a few days?'

'Ha. Did I not make it clear last night I'd welcome you with open ... arms.'

'Why I called.'

'Well then. Seven o'clock at mine, say. With a toothbrush.'

'That'll do nicely.'

He clicked off. Let any hacker pick the bones out of that. He glanced up, young trees, probably plane trees, lined this suburban road. Shadows from some of their leaves cast there by the young sun were dancing across his windscreen, almost bubbling. Yay! A nightingale was probably singing in Berkeley Square.

8

'HMMM ...?'

She had asked him something. He lay on his back staring at the hazy, not totally familiar ceiling as he tried to work out what the question might have been. With her head cradled on his left shoulder and her naked body tight against his it was not easy to come back from the serendipity to which his thoughts had floated. As his eyes brought the ceiling above back into immaculate whiteness, so his memory managed a focus of sorts.

'My pictures,' he said.

'I was merely observing that, given how well we've come to know each other these past few delicious hours, I've seen precious little of your original work. Virtually nothing, truth be told.'

'I trust, though, that what little you have experienced so far has proved, er, satisfactory.'

'Very much so, actually.'

'That's all good then. As to my pictures – well, there's not so much,' he said. 'And what there is is scattered pretty much in every direction.'

'Not at your place, then?'

'Only a couple. Hey! Hang about a minute.'

Prizing his left arm free from underneath her he scrunched over to the edge of his side of her double bed. Surely when she had triumphantly relieved him of his shirt such a short long time ago she had let it slip to the floor regardless so that his phone in the breast pocket, his racing mind had registered, had caused a not–to-be-worried-about-right-now thunk. Yes, correct! Here was the phone.

'I always forget,' he said. 'I've got my portfolio loaded on this.'

He wormed his way back against her and accessed the short file.

'Landscapes first,' he said. 'See what you think.'

She half-hoisted herself up so that her tightly plump breasts stretched provocatively close to his mouth. He resisted the urge to ask for 'afters'. After the best evening and small hours sex he had ever experienced he would not be such a fool as to court anti-climax. Instead he lay slightly uncomfortably propped up on his elbow looking at her looking at his work. He breathed through his mouth. A delicate aroma of the scent she wore had long since lost out to the good old-fashioned combination of male and female sweat blended at pressure. As he consciously inhaled its musky heaviness he noticed with approval how she took her time examining each painting, moving backwards as well as forwards through the file.

'I like this group,' she said at last, 'where did you do them?'

'Leith Hill and thereabouts.'

'Right. I particularly like this one. It's so open and enveloping. It makes you think of breezes and clean and wonderful English air.

'That's because of the vanishing point.'

'I don't see any vanishing point.'

'If you're standing in front of the canvas when it's hung the vanishing point is about fifty yards behind your shoulder blades.'

'Oh, of course! Ignorant me!'

'I actually managed to sell that one.'

'How?'

'Well, not so much my doing. There's a little shop-cum-gallery up the hill in Blackheath. I managed to get the woman who runs it to take a few canvasees on spec. That one found a home.'

'So it should have.'

She had flicked on to the portraits section. She had paused at his study of Jimmy Appleyard.

'This one's marvellous,' she said. 'What is it? Charcoal?'

'Pencil and ink.'

'Who is it?'

'Someone I was mates with in Ireland. Not in my regiment.'

'Do you still have it? It would –'

'I gave it to his widow.'

'Widow?'

'They were posted to Helmand. He bought it within weeks. An IED.'

'Ouch. But ...such a wonderful ... tribute.'

'She said so. She said she was going to have it framed properly. One day she said, she would show it to the child she was pregnant with to show him or her what their father had really been like.'

'What a tribute indeed!'

'Yes. I got quite choked up about that. That's why I'm so pissed off by your ex-brother-in-law. Jimmy was as straight and as true and as unselfish as they come.'

'That shows here. You've caught that.'

'Yes. One I got right. He was all that whereas Hilary Snot-face is nothing but self.'

'And self again. And then more self.'

'All the same ...'

'All the same what?'

'Well, if we run with the court case scenario ... what we think we've discovered might suggest ... the grimmest deduction ... Well, it's so blatant, so ... flagrant ... that you have –'

Cutting him off short with the violence of her movement Virginia Faulkner sat up beside him in the bed, and, oblivious of her nudity, glared down at him.

'That's it!' she exclaimed,' the whole bloody point! That bastard, the man who killed my sister has been brought up to lead an unbelievably privileged life. Led to believe the world's his oyster, his own fucking fiefdom to exploit just as he wants at any given moment. Born with a silver spoon. Daddy a Cabinet Minister, Eton, Oxford, sure party seat for the asking, he's never had a clue how the other half live. He spent his so-called adult life talking to judges in Pall Mall clubs, drinking with MPs on their Westminster Terrace. Chatting with Commissioners and civil servants and clergy in smoke-filled rooms. He's bribed, bent, cajoled and suborned his way forward. Don't even mentioned all the lobbyists he's cosied up to. Oiks like you and I don't even register on his radar. He's the sort who thinks he can rule any roost, wriggle out of any set-back and short-cut his way to whatever he wants on the strength of the £5,000 suit, a club tie and cut glass vowels. He's got no perspective, no scale, no sense of others. Flagrant is what he's all about.'

'You get flogged at Eton.'

'Only before you start dishing it out. He believes that because he went through the mill there early on he's paid his dues and is entitled to anything. He honestly believes that because everyone else is so beneath him he's above the law. He's arrogant to the point of blind stupidity!'

'He does have a BA.'

'In his case that only stands for Bullingdon Arsehole. Like many another MP we might think of he hasn't got a moral bone in his body.

'It would be instructive to meet with him one-on-one.'

'Whatever for?'

'To look into his non-existent soul.'

'All you'd see is a cruel, self-centred child.'

'I wonder if he'd fancy having his portrait painted ...'

'You're not serious?'

'Why not? Think he'd go for it?'

'Of course, he would. So long as it was a free offer. His ego would adore it. When it comes to flattery he's like Queen Victoria – you can't lay it on too thick ... but you daren't get that close to him, can you? Not after last night. It would be putting your head in the noose.'

9

ETHAN SHAW CAME INTO THE KITCHEN carrying what might have been a second chopping board to back up the one over which Virginia Faulkner was slaving.

His illusions and delusions apart,' he said, 'what form of address other than plain 'mister' is the man we love to hate entitled to?'

'None whatsoever,' Ginny replied, 'other than Prince Shitface. He's the plainest 'mister' that ever breathed air. Why do you ask?'

'I'm just dropping our said shitface that line,' Ethan Shaw said and left her to her chores.

Retiring to the cool, grey serenity of the living room he sat down on the two seater and juggling a sheet of plain A4 paper onto his balsa wood backing board and using a fountain pen he began to draft a letter. For some twenty minutes, exasperatingly grunting at intervals, he worked concentratedly away at the heart of the room's silence. As with a new grunt, this one of satisfaction, he finished his scribbling, the door opened and Ginny came in from the kitchen carrying two glasses of red wine.

'Five minutes,' she said.

'Timing. I've just finished. To whom should I be grateful for what I'm about to receive?'

'If you don't like it, Nigel Slater.'

He reached over the much corrected sheet of paper to her.

'See what you think,' he said.

She took the draft from him.

'Gosh you write well,' she said.

'Yes. But do I write well?'

'Let's see. Hey, you've put your real address at the top. Isn't that…'

'If our worst assumptions are correct it's not telling him anything he doesn't know already. I'm trying to suggest that I'm totally naïve and unsuspecting.'

'Yes. Maybe. Let me read all the rest.'

Dear Mr Paget-Bourke
This letter will come to you completely out of the blue, and the signature completing it will be visually at least, totally unfamiliar to you. Allow me then, please, to begin with some words of explanation / introduction.

I am an art student – a mature one, I am afraid, of 29 – in my last undergraduate year. My tastes and style are far more traditional than avant garde and I am proposing to advance my career along the traditional path of portraiture.

Some years ago our paths briefly crossed and I was struck then by what an interesting and challenging sitter for a portrait you might prove to be. (I can enlarge upon this as and when necessary). I am finally plucking up the courage formally to ask you whether there might be a possibility of my painting your portrait.

What I propose is this. I will execute an oil portrait for free. On its completion I will hand it over to you. If you detest it, you can destroy it at once as Clementine Churchill famously chose to do with Graham Sutherland's portrait of her husband Sir Winston. If, however, you like what I produce, it will be yours to hang up over your fireplace or in whatever other place you think best shows it to advantage. All I ask in return is that I may use photographs of the completed study subsequently to assist me in promoting my career (if any). So as not to trespass on your valuable time I would in all instances come to you – that is for preliminary sketches – two say – and subsequent progression on the main canvas – say three hours each – all these at any venue convenient for yourself.

Honour and common sense compel me to flag up one good

reason why you might wish to deny this unlooked for request. That occasion when our paths crossed was, alas, the inquest following your wife's motor accident. If my name rings a bell where my signature does not, it is because I was the other driver involved. The inquest, you will recall, totally absolved me of any guilt or blame in the incident and I very much hope that you have accepted such a verdict. However, my very presence may well serve to open old wounds and I have no wish at all to intrude on a private grief. I would quite understand if for this reason you might find my request impertinent.

Nevertheless, if only on the level of charity beginning at home, I would clearly be delighted if this rather oblique begging letter were to meet with your approval and hence a positive reply. Perhaps you will be kind enough to let me know of your decision in due course. Until then I remain, sincerely yours,

Ethan Shaw

Virginia Faulkner looked up and then laid the sheet of paper on the arm of her chair.

'What do you think?' Ethan Shaw asked.

'Deeply insincere, of course, but I don't think that shows through for anyone who doesn't know you in advance. A bit upmarket, I would say, which might put him on his guard. But you're offering him something classy – oils – for free and you're offering to stroke his ego. Should do the trick.'

'As long as it's only his ego.'

'All right. If you want to live dangerously I'll put this on the laptop and print it off.'

'O.K. Good. What are we eating?'

'See if you can guess.'

10

IN THE DAYS THAT FOLLOWED NOT only the despatch of his sales pitch letter to Paget-Bourke along with print-outs as well of the best examples of his portraiture work downloaded on to his smart phone, Ethan Shaw became first resigned and then inured to the mindless west-east slog across London from Hammersmith to Charlton.

Hammersmith was pure delight, Charlton was hard sledding – the setting for a student's pursuit of genius through the application of infinite pains. Hammersmith was good food, the cinema, a couple of concerts, an evening at the National Theatre and bed. Charlton was arriving at compositions where before there had been vacancy; was sharpening pencils; was discarding and trying again. Charlton was slog where Hammersmith was Ginny – forthright, sexy, quickly intelligent, supportive.

With Ginny to look forward to at the end of each day – and, with the help of a Penguin Joseph Conrad, he grew to blank out the time on the to and fro commute and rise to the needs of each return to his makeshift studio.

Central to his day now was his re-working – his re-doing – of his self-portrait. He began by re-familiarising himself with water colour by painting a simple fruit bowl still life. It might be simple, but he found the sheer doing of it deeply satisfying. And, when he was midway through it, granted him a huge reward.

Perhaps it was the greater fluency, the spontaneity of the water colour medium, the immediacy, that triggered the insight but he suddenly became aware that what his previous, now mutilated study had failed utterly to capture was the coincidence in the one image of his own past, present and future. If that was, given his having sent that letter, he still had a future. Well, at least he could now leave posterity an impression of how he'd foreseen himself at forty. Seeing that, he now had a conception of the portrait as it should be. Now all he had to do was do it. Well, onwards and upwards. He set out to make a start.

It was three weeks after they had posted the offer which he surely wouldn't refuse to Paget-Bourke that, arriving back at his flat yet again, Ethan Shaw found a stiffly expensive envelope addressed to him among the junk mail laid out to meet him in the carved-up house's minute entrance hall. Knowing what it was at once he opened the resisting envelope immediately before climbing the stairs. Yes! Matchingly expensive notepaper inside and typed, or rather printed out, a clean cut paragraph on portcullis-headed House of Commons stationary.

Dear Mr Shaw,
Please forgive me for the delay in replying to your kind and generous, if utterly expected – since unsolicited – offer to execute me. So to speak. I have only just returned to the UK from a brief but much needed holiday in Rhode Island.

Let me compensate for this tardiness by saying at once, 'Yes, why not?' In principle I am very willing to sit for you (I find your 'samples' interesting and compelling). Let us at least meet with a view to seeing how we may possibly pursue matters. I should warn you that while I possess a handful of very well thought of pictures, I myself, alas, can only be included amongst those many mortals who know nothing about Art except for knowing what they like when they see it. Perhaps indeed I shall like what I see of what you see in me.

Parliament, thank God, being currently in recess, I can now look forward to a few weeks here in Gloucestershire. This is from my point of view a very good time to get hold of me. Later on things will inevitably be more problematical. Perhaps you will be kind enough to liaise with my secretary as to when we might arrive at a mutually convenient date for an initial get together.

In the meantime my thanks for your interest. I look forward to meeting you.

Yours sincerely,

Hilary Paget-Bourke.

The expensively generated letter was over the flamboyant flourish of a fountain-penned signature whose calligraphy Ethan Shaw could only admire. The same pen had put a single stroke through the portcullis and written below Birchfield Hall. Yes, the envelope on further examination did not bear a stamp but had been franked by some internal –

'Beep.'

As he stood at the foot of the stairs taking in these details Ethan Shaw's thoughts were cut short by his smart phone. He fumbled it out from his shirt breast pocket.

'Hello?'

'Ethan Shaw?'

'Yes.'

'It's Alec here.'

'Alec?'

'As in Hillsborough was the pits. Does that –'

'Ah yes. Got you now.'

'I've come up with something might be grist to your mill.'

'Oh, satanic, then?'

'Possibly. Hence the cloak and dagger. Phones have ears, you know.'

'Right.'

'Can we meet?'

Coming and going on his way into and away from college Ethan Shaw had been aware of the Black Swan's existence and location for yonks. But, located a decent cover point's throw from

Deptford High Street, it was a pub he had never set foot in. Approaching it now at just gone nine this Thursday evening he found it unprepossessing that it was flush against its neighbouring buildings on this major route out of London and close to anonymous. All the same it sold beer. This would be the first time he had slept overnight in what he was obliged to call his own home in over three weeks. Not since the break-in. He wanted to have a few pints inside him before he settled down this night.

He pushed in through the pub's street door and at once his spirits rose. The Black Swan had not been gastro-gentrified within an inch of its life. It was reassuringly old-fashioned. Despite the drably nondescript exterior, trade seemed brisk. About twenty drinkers, all men - no, surely not – were scattered about the long bar and the various tables. The clientele's low mutter of conversation had not stopped or altered in pitch as he'd come in. Yes, this would do. If it quacked like a pub and smelt like a pub, it probably was a pub.

In the middle distance down along the counter one of the standing drinkers shifted his weight and by the slightest of movements signalled his presence. DI Bradley. As he moved towards him Ethan Shaw wondered whether it was a truism that over time all drinkers came to resemble the pub they regularly patronised.

'Evening,' Bradley said. 'Pint of ... ?'

'That'll do nicely.'

Ethan Shaw looked at the policeman. Plain clothes and then some. The same faded into colourlessness suit, the same tie. Probably the same shirt. Now, though, as well, an unbuttoned raincoat neither fawn nor grey, the perfect apparel for a dedicated flasher. Fresh from the struggle to render his own matt-finished yet high-light reflecting skin tones in paint, Ethan Shaw glanced at Bradley's tired, seamed features and, as they turned to catch the barman's eye, was struck by their over-riding characteristic. The skin seemed dusty. Bradley seemed tired, disillusioned and past it because he seemed in want of a good brushing down. 'Watch it!' something clicked in his own mind: coming across as dreary was probably Bradley's chief professional asset.

'This your local?' Ethan Shaw asked.

'Not geographically,' Bradley said .'But in effect, yes. A copper's pub. About six of us in here right now. Handy for the nick, you see, and the magistrate's court around the corner. Best place for you and me to meet. The others will all think I'm tapping up a new grass.'

'Charming.'

'Takes all sorts, grassing does.'

The barman had pulled the pint.

'Cheers,' Ethan Shaw said gratefully.

'Cheers ... Now – I've managed to dig up something on that Reynolds. Long story short – I was in touch with a friend of a friend. Seems you're dead right – he's one of the genuinely rotten apples.'

'Yes?'

'Yes. Seems he jumped before he was pushed. Just before. A long held reputation for cosying up to west country villains etcetera; for having several 'ghosts' on his own grass roster. Blind eye if you paid for one. Then, your suspicion to one side, a real biggy.'

'Oh?'

'Huge drugs bust in Bristol. Street value of gadzillions if you cut it right. Then – hey presto – the stuff was all gone missing. Just not there anywhere anymore. Guess who was seconded to St Paul's at just that time.'

'I can't begin to.'

'Well, yes he was. Cast iron cover story, of course, but nobody had any real doubts. He was a dead cert for being asked to move on. Then – hey presto once again – there he was gone. Jumped ship just in the nick.'

'To go to Paget-Bourke.'

'Right.'

' He must have seen it coming.'

'Oh certainly. His sort always makes a point of having dirt on the bosses. He'd have got it across that if he went down big he'd do a lot of talking. A lot of dead bodies would have certainly sat up in old graves. Somebody, singular or plural, tipped him off to go while the going was still possible. Full pension still on and all. A nice clean break as far as Internal would be concerned. No names. No mess. No scandal.'

'So he blackmailed a job out of Paget-Bourke.'

'Well, yes and no. He certainly knew what he knew. But no way he could bring Pagett-Brown down. Oh, that one definitely bats for the other side by the way. No, Reynolds could hardly bring his new boss down without fingering himself, could he? On a really serious charge. No plea bargaining there. No, what I reckon, is that they realise they are stuck with one another now. 'You don't tell, I don't tell'. Must make for a very edgy time when they are together. Both protecting their own back like buggery.'

'So to speak.'

'I don't hear that's on for Reynolds.'

'Right. Even edgier, then for his alleged boss.'

'Yeah.'

'The other half?'

So long as it's a pint.'

Ethan Shaw caught the barman's eye. In no time at all their glasses were full again.

'Thanks,' Bradley said. 'Cheers.'

'Cheers.'

'Look, are you planning to go ahead with your little private investigation?'

'Maybe.'

'Well in that case, a word to the wise. Keep an eye on Reynolds too. He's devious and vicious with it. And he's got just as much to lose as his boss.'

'He's just as guilty. But thanks. I'll bear all that in mind.'

'Be a good idea.'

'In that connection there's another favour I would like to ask of you.'

A further exchange of pints later, Ethan Shaw stood at the stop just along from the Black Swan waiting for the first of his two buses home. He felt on the verge of shivering. There was a hint of chill in the air, the first he'd been aware of in ages. Autumn wasn't so far away. He'd come out for the evening under-dressed and, yes, now he had gone right ahead and shivered. Bradley had been right about that raincoat. This would be his first night alone since the break-in but, he told himself, it was not such a big thing. In his first week of day-tripping back to work in his studio he had sacrificed one afternoon to going along to a B&Q and buying the two elementary but stonking bolts which he'd fitted to the inside of his own front door. The door itself would cave in any time the big bad wolf chose to huff or puff, but the bolt would delay the entry and create enough noise in the process to have him out of bed and, hammer in hand, remembering his unarmed combat training. Not that that was likely to be called upon. Apart from bracing Ayers he had amused himself by planting a few James Bondish scotch tape traps each evening before sloping off to Hammersmith. None of them had ever been disturbed on his return the next morning.

All the same, as he turned into his street, everything seemed as quiet as the grave and by the time he'd climbed the stairs and let himself in, the studio-cum-flat seemed not only cold and dark but lonely too. Unpopulated. Its corners and shadows were darker than he remembered.

The beer had made him peckish but his cupboard was bare. He

picked up the Conrad and read for a while until he was persuaded he felt tired. Then he went to bed.

He found he wasn't tired at all: and yes, once again, his ears were pricked, alive to the slightest change in audio input from inside or outside the house. It was impossible to switch off. It was amazing how much noise there could be on a night of utter silence. He began to think of Ginny. Was she having trouble sleeping too? Did her house all that way there across London suddenly seem underpopulated as well? He had given her points for all sorts of admirable qualities – him and her, it wasn't just the sex – but he knew one of the things that bound him to her was in the minus column, her vulnerability. It wasn't obvious – she hid it well – but he was certain she still grieved for her sister, still mourned for her. The brisk, contemptuous hatred she felt for Paget-Bourke was fuelled by that sense of bereavement. He himself had been the unwitting agent of that death. He owed the survivor.

Light was trying to drill through his eyelids. He became aware that the increasing pressure on his system to pee was dragging him awake. All that beer last night. Well, here was morning after all: night had passed all the long way through and he hadn't dreamed a thing.

On the way to the loo he checked his watch. Ouch. Twenty to nine. Late. He was almost out of Prussian Blue.

11

THE BIG VAUXHALL SWUNG OFF THE narrow country road and in through the seemingly always open gates of Birchfield Hall. It proceeded crunchingly up the gravelled driveway. Seated pompously, as it felt, in the car's rear Ethan Shaw stared past the head of his elderly chauffeur and watched the house, seriously confident in its classic proportions, float steadily towards him through the windscreen. Danger would never have worn so unassuming a face.

'Where would you like me to halt, sir?' his driver asked.

'Right outside the front door,' Ethan Shaw said. 'Pull over on to the apron there.'

Well he wasn't a tradesman, was he? Even if he was about to pretend that he was.'

'Very good, sir.'

The saloon went through a curvy ninety degrees and came to a halt level with the house's front door.

'And of course I'll need my bag,' Ethan Shaw said.

'Yes sir,' his driver said respectfully making clear his irritation at such redundant instruction.

The two men got out of the vehicle simultaneously. Ethan Shaw went not to the house's front door but to the car's rear, where, as he had engineered, his hired driver was unlocking the boot and, after a brief pause, getting out the large canvas satchel he had been earlier asked to stow away there.

'Thank you,' Ethan Shaw said slinging the satchel's strap over his shoulder. 'Twelve o'clock, then.'

The driver duly nodded.

'Yes sir,' he said, 'twelve.'

He began to return to his driver's seat while, going his separate way, Ethan Shaw headed toward the house door.

He had ascended all three of the shallow steps up to the house and had his right arm raised when, abruptly, the door was opened in his face. Before him, dressed in a black suit, the man he knew to be called Reynolds, stared at him impassively across the threshold.

'Yes?' Reynolds said.

'Mr Shaw for Mr Paget-Bourke,' Ethan Shaw said. 'I have an appointment for ten o'clock.'

Reynolds acknowledged this claim. As the car made itself heard scrunching through a three point turn his eyes switched away from their unblinking person to person stare and registered the manoeuvre.

'George Standish, Cheltenham Car Hire,' he said dismissively.

'Correct,' Ethan Shaw said.

Reynolds made his dour purposely expressionless gaze personal again. He was the sort of old sweat NCO who, while not technically outranking you, in working practice looks down on you from below.

'I'll let Mr Paget-Bourke know you've arrived,' Reynolds said at last. Uncivilly, with no invitation to the guest to enter, he turned on his heel and walked away. Ethan Shaw closed the front door upon himself. A mistake he thought to himself, a mistake. He didn't show the least surprise: not even a flash of recognition. They were expecting me. So.

He looked about him. The hall surprisingly small, except where in line with the front door it receded away in a passage to an internal door, was tiled in white marble tiles which, each bearing a small black rectangle in its four corners, were butted up together to create an emphatic black square where they met to thus form a pleasing Italianate impression. Pleasing, Ethan Shaw felt, but not quite appropriate to the house's original period. Better was the staircase to the left of the receding passageway. A rich burgundy carpet swept royally down over what looked like oak treads and was echoed by a bannister rail burnished by time and painstaking servants to a magnificently glowing – even in this reduced light – ruby patina. The hall and passage were devoid of furniture and ornament but now, as the further door reopened, were occupied by the returning Reynolds.

'Mr Paget-Bourke knows you're here,' he said. He opened a door parallel to Ethan Shaw's right hand. 'He'd like you to wait in here.'

Churlish to the end. The man's voice was as thickset as his physique. It seemed not to carry the slightest indication of any regional source but only indicated urban, lower-class origins. Oh Christ, Ethan Shaw thought, I've grown up to be an elitist.

'Right,' he as brusquely replied and went through the door into the front room. It was a fine room, not large but in its extension back from two front windows towards the house rear, long and thin. A neat, not overlarge marble fireplace caught the eye as it thrust forward its flat planes and minimum roundels the instant you came in through the door and before it at oblique angles stood two Victorian armchairs reupholstered in a modern steel-blue fabric. The walls were covered with a vertically striped paper in modestly subdued shades of olive and old gold suggestive of graciousness and times past; landscape pictures of green fields and quiet rivers hung on the interior wall. The thrust of the chimney breast created alcoves on its either side. In the one a splendid, folded shut Regency card table outdid the staircase bannister with the swirled patterning of its glowing grain. On its top making a royal blue punctuation point stood a splendid porcelain bowl. The other alcove sheltered a delicate writing desk of about the same period, which was extended down to reveal the intricacy of its many sub-divided compartments. Nice, Ethan Shaw thought, very nice. As he worked the satchel from off his shoulder he braced himself. Whatever else his purpose – and what was it anyway? – he must give this occasion its due and his best shot. He must take it seriously, treat it as if it were the real thing. Now then ... how to make use of this background? Exploit the room.

Moving towards the soft light let in by the windows he considered the view beyond. A handsome expanse of lawn a little less than formal but respectfully acknowledging the house. The grey-white ribbon of the gravelled driveway leading back to the gate. Fine trees, tall and currently noble in an autumnal way planted across from the drive and within the perimeter of the red-rose wall. It was indeed a view to die, or, if need be, kill for.

Yes, here. Just where he stood now. He turned and walked across to the bowl and flicked his right index finger at its rim. Perhaps the response would ring out true as to whether the bowl was Ming or Tang. He had just discovered it was of the Chunk period when the door behind him opened and, turning, he was looking straight at his respective client.

'So sorry to have kept you,' Hilary Paget-Bourke said. 'I've just been stuck with Westminster on the line. The Home Office. They are so intent on having the last word, it's a work of art to get them to hang up.'

He uses that all the time, Ethan Shaw thought.

'Talking of which – hello!'

Paget-Bourke took a step further into the room, his right arm extended. Proffering his own hand Ethan Shaw met him halfway. Neither limp-wristed nor a crushing attempt at power play the handshake, he thought, might be fairly described as a free and frank exchange of greetings. He bent to retrieve his satchel and when he straightened found his alleged subject to be had taken up a position dead in front of the fireplace.

Whew! Hilary Paget-Bourke was handsome and then some. It would be virtually impossible to find oneself accused of laying it on too thick if complimenting him on his good looks to his face. He must have stood an even six feet tall and was slender with it – not skinny but lithe. He possessed a perfect posture, erect, shoulders pressing back that still succeeded in looking relaxed and at ease in their uprightness. But it was his features that drew the eye. They were classically perfect. You had to think of Greek statues. He looked like an actor who had been rejected for the role of the young Rupert Brooke on the grounds that he was too good looking.

He was fair of face and of hair. The face was slightly more oval than round and dominated by twin cheek bones that stretched the unblemished skin taut across themselves with a Slavic intensity. A perfect slender nose, long but neither hooked nor concave, ran downwards to divide the cheekbones and lead the eye to the balancingly wide thin-lipped mouth above a narrowing crisply pointed chin. The face shone with health as did the hair. Parted conventionally on the left side and brushed casually straight back, the hair shone with a natural gleam that owed nothing to a bottle. The artful non-styling of the hair was the one aspect of Paget-Bourke's appearance that lacked symmetry. Otherwise he was one of the rare individuals whose profiles, right and left, formed mirror images of each other. The hair, in fact, saved him from seeming a stylised mannequin rather than a young Apollo.

The hair, that was, and as well the eyes. The eyes might once have been a pale shade of blue. Time since, however, seemed to have diluted that shade to a washed-out bluish-grey. They were the eyes, Ethan Shaw thought to think, of certain hawk-eyed super sportsmen he could recall; the eyes of an actor chosen to play the key bit part of the cold blooded gunslinger. The eyes lent their owner character. Character that would have to be dealt with.

'Right!' Paget-Bourke had clapped his long, slender hands together in the way he would have employed at many a committee meeting.

'Here we are,' he said. 'Just remind me first of the rules of engagement, the rules of the game. You propose to paint my portrait entirely free of charge ...?'

'Yes. That's what I said – or meant to say – in my letter. I undertake to produce a finished portrait. In oils. When it's finished I shall make you a present of it. It will be yours to keep or destroy as you think fit.'

'So what's in it for you, then?'

'All I ask is the right to photograph the end result and, if I choose, include it in any portfolio of work I might put together to secure new commissions.'

'Right. Reasonable enough. But why pick on me?'

'Two reasons – neither of which enable me to spare your blushes. One is that you are a figure of some eminence, very much in the public eye.'

'Potentially I'll be good bait.'

'Yes. If you want to put it that way.'

'Well let's hope my future career doesn't put all that into reverse.'

Or not, Ethan Shaw thought.

'Reason number two?'

'When our paths crossed – however unhappily, however tragic the circumstances – I was immediately struck by the thought that you would make a wonderful sitter, subject for a portrait.'

'Well really, I–'

'It's not just a question of good looks,' Ethan Shaw hastily kept on. 'It's that you're so patrician in appearance and demeanour. You see, I think I wrote that I'm a very traditional artist.'

'Not Picasso, eh?'

'Alas, no.'

'None of that 'a word in your nose' stuff is what I mean.'

So the Philistine sod had never seen Pablo's 'Stein'.

'Not at all. One of my heroes is Gainsborough. I see in you a chance to link this age back to his world of aristocrats. While there is still time. Frankly your own type is a disappearing breed.'

'An endangered species?'

'Exactly. I'd like to catch it on the wing. Preserve it in oil.'

'Hmmm ... Very flattering, I'm sure. I'd have thought that in that regard you'd make a good subject for a portrait yourself. If you don't mind my saying so you have quite an air about you that attracts.'

If only you knew, Ethan Shaw thought. Well maybe he does.

'Thank you but I'm not the Gainsborough type,' he said.

'Not married?'

'Not yet.'

'Ah, haven't yet found the lady who can keep you in the manner to which you have become accustomed, eh?' Paget-Bourke said.

Bastard, Ethan Shaw thought.

At that moment, right on cue his smart phone rang.

'Damn!' he pretended. 'Excuse me a second.'

'Of course.'

Ethan Shaw took the phone from out the vest pocket of his work shirt.

'Hello,' he said.

'In the lion's den?' DI Bradley asked. 'All well?'

'Indeed.'

'Good. Your turn,' Bradley said.

'Look, we've done all this,' Ethan Shaw snapped back. 'I gave you a sample over a week ago.'

'I have to tell you it's been contaminated,' Bradley parroted.

'Oh for God's sake! If I give you another who's to tell me that won't end up contaminated too?'

'Temper, temper.'

'Look this isn't at all convenient right now. I'm miles out of London at this moment as it happens with a client.'

'His nibs, eh?'

'I won't be back home till late in the afternoon.'

'Whereabouts are you?'

'A place called Birchfield.'

'Where?'

'Birchfield. Near Cheltenham. It's just a village.'

'Well give us a call when you get back.'

'I'll give you a call when I get back. That's my best offer.'

Affecting bad temper he snapped the phone off.

'Jumped up jack,' he muttered.

'Trouble?' Paget-Bourke languidly enquired.

'Bloody police. Excuse my French. I had my flat turned over by burglars a couple of weeks ago.'

'Oh, nasty. Very nasty. Did –'

'I was out at the time or it might have been. The police took a DNA sample from me so they could 'eliminate me from any enquiries' – me! The one who called them in! Now they've obviously lost it. And it's pointless anyway. I'm sorry. I should have turned the phone off the moment I arrived.'

'Well you have now. How did you get down here?'

'I didn't want to get here frazzled from an endless drive. I got the quick train down to Cheltenham. Then I got a hired car. He's going to pick me up at The Fox at midday.'

For the first time a frown qualified Paget-Bourke's smooth forehead and a cloud gathered in the depths of his ultra-pale eyes.

'Really,' he said. 'I had hoped to entertain you to a bit of kitchen lunch *chez moi*. Just a cold collation but with a decent bottle.'

'That's a very kind thought,' Ethan Shaw hastily interrupted,' and in the normal way I would have accepted like a shot – very useful for me, you know, combining business with pleasure. But sod's law is there is something I have to get back to London for this evening. Alas I'll have to pass.'

'I get tired of my own company lunchtimes down here in the sticks,' Paget-Bourke grumbled. 'But, very well – if needs must, we'd better crack on with it. How do you see me dressed? This lot a bit too casual, I assume.'

'I gather then you're accepting my offer,' Ethan Shaw said.

'Why not? What have I got to lose?'

'Well your time perhaps. Thank you very much. It's really generous of you and I do appreciate it,' Ethan Shaw said while considering Paget-Bourke's dress. In fact it was entirely suitable.

The subject to be was wearing a dark blue double breasted blazer over designer jeans. And dark blue suede loafer shoes. He wore a vermilion coloured pullover beneath the blazer and at the shallow v-neck a fleck of red in the pattern of a tattersall shirt made a neat match.

'Well,' Ethan Shaw said while thinking wildly and literally on his feet, 'what you're wearing now will do nicely, to coin a phrase.'

Mentally thanking the absent Bradley for putting words in his mouth, he stooped down and took out a big sketch book and back board from his tote bag.

'It's too casual for Gainsborough in his day and age,' he went on, 'but just right for me. Here and now. What I had in mind – Look, would you be kind enough to walk over to that left-hand side window and look out at the lawn.'

Not replying Paget-Bourke did as he'd been told.

'What I had in mind was a three-quarter length standing pose – to show off your height – and, good, this is getting there – can you turn your head, your head only, please, and look more towards the driveway. Yes, good.

'What I thought was three-quarter length, three-quarter profile.'

Not altogether to his surprise Ethan Shaw realised indeed he was giving this subterfuge encounter his very best artistic shot.

'Are you going to photograph me here?' Paget-Bourke said.

'No, no. The phone's lens never gets the perspective right. Oh, I'll take some stills as an aide memoir – the room, the wall, the window, even your face. But I won't just copy any one-off photo-image.'

'I should apologise, I imagine,' Paget-Bourke said. 'The camera does lie. It's the painter who reveals the window to the soul.'

If only you knew, mate.

'Actually it's more that the camera doesn't tell enough of the truth. You see this is what I have in mind. I want to convey three ages. First there's you in the prime of life here in the present. You're looking out through the window. But you are also contemplating the future. But also, you're looking at the future from where your predecessor stood, from out of the past. I want to try to combine all those three time zones in the one image.'

Jesus, Ethan Shaw thought, I'm allowing him to look into my own soul.

'Very ingenious,' Paget-Bourke said, 'But maybe a touch ambitious?'

'True. But I am going to try to go for it.'

Dragging what was actually a dining chair from its corner to where he judged his eyeline should be, Ethan Shaw set himself down, crossed his right leg over his left and began his initial sketch.

Perhaps because he had no final reason to believe the exercise was for real, perhaps because he was as much concerned with his own safety as his subject, he had never worked better. The light was good, the pose was good, the charcoal was darting over the paper with a mind of its own.

'I'll cheat the background a bit,' he heard himself say. 'I'll bring the alcove behind you further forward to establish the scale. And in it, with your permission, I'll paint a picture of the house itself on the wall behind you. The front seen from outside. That way the thinking viewer will clock that the picture is about time. The present between the past and the future.'

'Very neat,' Paget-Bourke said.

Such a perfect voice! High in register but somehow reverberant. A royal accent but clean cut. That was it! This was another person who talked like he looked.

'Mind you,' Paget-Bourke said, 'you don't object to me talking?'

'No, no. Not at all.'

'Speaking personally regarding the past, I don't think Gainsborough would have stooped to painting my forebears.

'As far as I've ever bothered to enquire, I believe I'm from pretty mongrel stock. It was poor dear Angela who brought the blue blood into Birchfield. She was distantly, obliquely somehow, descended from the de Beauforts.'

There you could go. Hilary Paget-Bourke was just plain folks and modest with it. Or not.

'You must miss her very much,' Ethan Shaw risked.

'Not a day goes by that I don't think about her.'

Well that, of course, could be taken two ways.

'Speaking personally again, mind you,' Paget-Bourke went on, 'I have always concentrated my efforts on becoming an ancestor rather than a descendant.'

Ethan Shaw discovered his charcoal had skipped a beat. He repaired the gap.

'How do your daughters manage these days?' he said.

Paget-Bourke was silent for a moment and Ethan Shaw felt that he had overdone it. Perhaps he had merely seemed impertinent.

'Well enough, I fancy,' Paget-Bourke said. 'They know their mama has gone to live with Jesus in Heaven, of course, but they adore their Nanny. They've just gone off back to boarding school again. That keeps their minds off things.'

How fucking convenient.

'Sometimes they can get a little downcast. But they are only little girls after all. Little women. It doesn't take much in the way of pretty presents to buck them up again.'

Bastard in spades and doubled!

Hatching in loose areas of shade he tried to remain expressionless.

'There!' he was able to say after a while, 'that's me done.'

'Already?'

'For the moment.'

'May I see?'

'Of course.'

Breaking his pose Paget-Bourke came across and looked over Ethan Shaw's shoulder.

'I say,' he said. 'That's really rather good. It's very good, in fact. Excellent.'

It was too.

'You can, of course, have this as well in due course.'

'Thank you very much.'

'Immediately, I need it to work from.'

'Ah, that raises a point I should perhaps have brought up earlier. How many more sittings do you envisage?'

'Two probably. Certainly one. And much longer than this.'

'Yes ... well ... Parliament reconvenes next week. I shall need to be going up to town in a couple of days.'

'Well if I were a well-established painter we would meet up again at my studio. But as things are ... Where do you live in London?'

'Close to the Embankment at present. No, not on a bench. Just now I've a *pied à terre* flat in Godolphin Square. Does that mean anything to you?'

'Just. I know where it is. I've never had occasion to visit it. Can we meet there?'

'I don't see why not.'

'I can do the background setting here from photographs. I'll bring lots of plastic so your carpet won't end up looking like a Jackson Pollock.'

'Excellent then. I'll have Reynolds give you my London details.'

'Sorry, who?'

'Reynolds, my man of all work.'

'Oh yes, of course.'

'Gainsborough and Reynolds,eh? Are you sure I can't tempt you with something? I've got some very nice French cider.'

'No, thanks but no thanks. It's very kind of you but I'd best be on my way. I've got this thing and, if I can squeeze it in, I'd best try and keep the boys in blue happy and out of my face.'

'Always a good idea.'

Ethan Shaw studiously repacked his satchel.

'I have to say, speaking for myself, I'm delighted with today. For me it's been a great success and a great pleasure too.'

'Good. And for me too. I've enjoyed it as well. It's been instructional, should I say? I'll just find Reynolds, if you'll excuse me'

Paget-Bourke bore his glamour-puss and almost colourless eyes before him out of the room. Ethan Shaw completed his packing wondering which of the two of them was the more two-faced. He had been left, he suddenly realised completely alone once again. He took out his smart phone and switched it back on. Swiftly he reeled off close-ups in the room; the wallpaper, the ceramic bowl, the window frames, the card table ... Yes, enough. Still no-one had come. Time was now crawling by. Ah, the door was opening.

Reynolds came into the room.

'Mr Paget-Bourke sends his apologies,' he said dourly. 'He's been trapped on the phone again. He asked me to wish you a 'safe home' on his behalf and to send you on your way.'

As in 'escort off the premises'.

Reynolds held out a small card.

'He asked me to give you this – his London address.'

'Excellent. Thank you.' Ethan Shaw took the card. 'Before I go I just have to take a photograph of the front of the house.'

'Yes. Fine.'

Reynolds lead him into the hall and down the shallow steps to the outside world. Ethan Shaw dumped his satchel on the gravelled forecourt and walked quickly to the centre of the lush but finely manicured grass at the front of the house. Reynolds made no effort to remove himself from the composition but that was a detail. Ethan Shaw took three pictures of the house. Moving more slowly back across the grass he diligently mimed making a call on the phone. When he returned to his satchel he found Reynolds was standing four-squarely beside it.

'I understand you're heading for The Fox,' he said. 'I'd be happy to give you a lift if it would be a help.'

Ethan Shaw tried not to be seen hesitating. So far today, so good. Yes, go for it.

'That would be great,' he said.

12

AGAIN! THE MOMENT THE TRAFFIC STREAMING eastwards towards his windscreen had jumped into oncoming focus and then begun blurring by to his right the rational part of his dream consciousness knew from the *déjà vu* that his nightmare documentary was not yet a thing of the past. He sensed part of his brain steeling itself and his nerves tightening in a fearful pre-knowledge. Yes, here it came once more, The Countryman was skittering across the dividing line into the suicide (but never suicide) alley and on towards his cab and, once again, there was nothing he could do to avoid the inevitable. But no! Something had altered. This was different.

As the Mini straightened to hurtle at him head on, as his muscles stiffened in his sleep, he became aware of a dead centre to his vision. This time the doomed driver was not sawing hysterically at her wheel. She was sitting motionless staring with fixed resignation at her implacable fate. And her hair had changed colour. She had changed. It was a different person. It wasn't Angela Faulkner but her sister Virginia! Ginny!

'Ugh!'

Mini-seconds before the impact would convulse his dreamscape Ethan Shaw sat bolt up in bed, his heart hammering, his lungs gaspingly sucking in air, icy sweat running down his chest, his taut arm and leg muscles jerking uncontrollably.

'Ethan! What is it!' Virginia cried out.

It was the middle of the night and he was still in the double bed in Hammersmith.

'Nightmare,' he somehow spluttered out through his locked throat. 'That dream.'

A more intense iciness was suddenly flushing through his whole being. Consciousness, logic, was making him a coward. The variation to the dream was telling him how terrible and desolate a place the world would be if Ginny was no longer part of it.

'Terrible,' he managed to mumble. 'Awful.'

'Shsh,' Ginny said. 'It's all right. It was only your dream. Shush.'

'Different,' he said. 'This time it was you driving. You I hit.'

Ginny rolled towards him and softly warm and firm clasped herself yieldingly to the entire length of his naked body.

'I'm here,' she said. 'Alive. Very much alive. Feel my feeling you. It was just a bad dream. Dreams don't count.'

'It was terrible,' he said. 'You and not her. For no reason. For every reason, I thought. It was an icy dread. Icy.'

She reached her hand down between his legs. Since they had been making love earlier that night she was naked too. He had been limp there, flaccid, unmanned by the iciness. But now she was caressing him, coaxing him.

'I'm here beside you. Alive, unhurt, warm. Let me make you warm again too.'

Langorously she squirmed her way across and on top of him. He felt her warm, gentle breathing on the side of his neck. Then she was kissing him steadily.

He had never before in his life had that sense of potential bereavement over a girl.

'This is what's real,' she said.

They were one flesh again. The universe was flesh again. For a long time they kept it like that. Finally they rolled apart.

'Late in tomorrow,' she said.

'Better now,' he replied. 'Not cold anyhow.'

They lay on their backs staring at the ceiling.

'Why do you think T.E. Lawrence changed his namel?' she suddenly said.

'To Shaw? So he could get lost in the crowd, I suppose. As names go it's pretty anonymous.

'Mrs Shaw does seem a bit commomplace,' she said, 'but I'm sure I could get used to it.'

He stiffened.

'Are you saying what I think you're saying?' he said.

'Yes.'

'You wouldn't believe it if I told you I was just thinking the same thing, would you?' he said.

'Yes,' she said. 'After tonight I would.'

The better to look at her he rolled onto his side. 'Perhaps we should then,' he said.

'Yes,' she said for the third time.

'Then here's to you, Mrs S,' he said

'It's Shaw, remember. Not Robinson.

'Hey, hey, hey,' he duly replied.

He nudged his way closer and gently kissed her. Rolling aside at last he gave way to a deep, rich, contented laugh.

'What's so funny?'

'I was just wondering how many marriage proposals are made in warm beds between people without any clothes on and their eyes open.'

'Thinking about it, I'd say quite a lot, wouldn't you?' she said.

It was not until his second, his after the toast, cup of coffee that he returned to the topic.

'So,' he said. 'Your decision of last night ... you still sticking to it?'

'Naturally. Why ever not.'

'Second thoughts are often wiser.'

'A gorgeous hunk with a mind of his own? What's not to like?'

'The almost certainty of future poverty?'

'Let me worry about that. No, I'm not following in the footsteps of Miss Austen.'

Of what?'

'Jane Austen. It seems staying at the stately home of some acquaintance she one evening accepted a proposal of marriage from one of the household's filthy rich sons. Next morning she told him, 'Thanks but no thanks.''

'Cold feet?

'I fancy she thought him too close to her own Mr Collins.'

'Who?'

'The odiously complacent clergyman Elizabeth Bennett turns down in *Pride and Prejudice*.'

'Oh, yeah.'

'So you are still in the frame. I'll hold you to it.'

'Good. We've achieved something positive at least.'

'Meaning what?'

'Well, as regards little Lord Fauntleroy we've run into a brick wall, haven't we?'

'Have we?'

'Well, after my little visit, no question he's gay – he lost no time before trying to come on to me – and his views on women are obviously loathsome. But in this day and age neither of those things is a crime.'

'They are, both, let me repeat, political suicide.'

'For a wannabe leader,yes. But I reckon I was stupid. I went charging down a cul-de-sac and kicked over a wasps' nest.'

'You reckon?'

'Yes. His nibs has so much ego, he might, just might, have sailed for the grease job I lavished on him. But not Reynolds. He knows we know. Those few minutes when he was giving me a lift to the pub were poisonous. I was so glad my ride was already waiting. The ball is back in their court now. They will be the pair looking to get on the front foot. At this pair's expense.'

'There is the little matter of him having killed my sister.'

'Yes. Cynically. Bloody mindedly. At the risk of killing God knows how many others.'

''At the risk of killing you!'

'Yes. All right. But what can we do from here? We can't get a Parliamentary bill up and running, can't engineer a court case. We're not going to kill them in cold blood, are we?'

'In tepid maybe ...'

'No. That would be tacky.'

'I suppose ... Look, I think I'm going to call a sickie today. Take the whole day off. I haven't done it once so far so you can say they owe me.'

'OK. I really ought to go back over and crack on with the masterpiece. We'll go out tonight and celebrate, think up names for babies.'

'Lovely. How's it coming anyway?'

'The masterpiece? Very well ironically. It's because I'm doing it fast.'

'I'd love to come over and see it.

'Not a good idea. A: my pad is a complete and utter tip. B: I've got a nasty sixth sense someone's keeping an eye on me there, It's all right during the day but as of now they don't know we're a pair. Best keep it that way.

'Makes sense, I suppose,'

'Anyway – I've got the current state of the portrait on my phone. Look.'

Downing the last of his coffee he fished out his mobile and accessed its photo section. He handed the image across the table.

'It's brilliant. It's him to the squalid life! He looks like a Jesus in the Wilderness who has just accepted all the kingdoms of the earth from Satan.'

'Well, after a shave. But thanks.'

Because she obviously was too, he felt thrilled. He smiled his thanks towards her. But already she was pensive again.

'I suppose. If they are not plotting against each other they might be working on a counter attack,' she said.

'Well, Reynolds almost certainly.'

'But we've not quite run out of road, have we?'

'No?'

'No. There's that ex-boyfriend with his passport and his letters.'

'Well ...'

'And there's me. I'm my nieces' godmother. That's got to give me some rights.'

Across the marmalade and crumbs they looked at each other with a wild surmise.

Quite later on that same afternoon Ethan Shaw found himself standing alone in his tip of a Charlton studio-cum-flat and staring at his current work in progress, the portrait of Hilary Paget-Bourke. It was well advanced. He would be losing the light before too much longer. It made sense to work on something self-evidently brief and to the point. Yes, he would set about adding in the imaginary picture of Birchfield Hall on the wall of the alcove behind the composition's main subject.

If he had been using a camera then, more than likely, an actual painting of the house hanging in that position would have photographed slightly out of focus. But he was not a photographer; that was the whole point. He was seeking to fuse those three ages. The image of the house represented the last. It required being depicted as firmly and inescapably as the key moments in everybody's past are lodged home in the mind. He needed to limn the house in with maximum precision.

He walked over to the plasterer's table he used as a work-bench and rummaging around among his knives and wedges laid hands on his maul stick. God, it was heavy! It was not actually a purpose-designed maul stick but a longish ebony cylindrical rod, a Victorian ledger-clerk's ruler, which he had picked up for a song in a Greenwich junk shop. It was ages since he had used it, but it did a job and would do so again now.

He crossed back towards his easel. Doing so, he passed the bedroom's big window and from habit glanced out. He stopped short. A movement in the road below had caught his eye. Forty yards along a big man with reddish-auburn hair was getting into a parked car – the newcomer Seat that had turned up in the last week or so. Remaining at the window he grabbed a rag and mimed rubbing the maul stick clean as, covertly he continued to eyeball the car. Bingo! As he watched a hand came out of the side window and repositioned the rear-view mirror. Ah! Idiot! The car was a left-hand drive model. As a painter he was supposed to have an eye for detail and yet he had only just clocked that it was a left-hanger. He risked another direct look. The car was downstream from his window and across the road but he could make out that the wing mirror of, yes, the driver's door was showing a pinky-grey. The driver's reflected face. Yes, the mirror was slanted to look directly back towards his flat. A left-hand drive Seat most like from sunny Spain. Now there was food for thought.

Strangely gathered he returned to his easel. No need to render the pointing slavishly. Subtly different tone to the brickwork would imply that. But the window frames were important. They must give four-square insight and witness to a rational age when people thought they knew what they could see going on right in front of their noses. He went back to his bench and sought out his white ink. Chummy was still behind the sinister wheel – busting, it was to be hoped, for his post-pub pee. He dipped a thin nib into the ink. The maul stick supported his right hand perfectly. It might have to do another job before the day, the oncoming night, were over.

Gone four o'clock. So had the best of the light. A good time to stop. Save the slate roof for later. Easy enough to do. The picture within the picture was otherwise done. He cleaned his brushes and then - glancing at the wing mirror, yes fine – went down the stairs and out. Turning left he crossed the road and walked past the Seat and the auburnish shade on the edge of vision. Thirty strides further on he heard what he had been expecting – the 'clunk' of a closing car door.

He did not walk far. Three streets further on, at a corner with what served as a main feeder road for the enclave of terraced houses was a cheap and cheerful barber's shop. He strode through the door without looking back and found both the two chairs were unoccupied. A barber, barely out of his teens, his own footballer's coiffeur scarcely an advertisement for his skills, rose up from behind a copy of the Metro and looked the obvious question.

'Just a tidy up,' Ethan Shaw said.

Already holding clippers in his hand, the youth was hesitating.

'You a number one or a two?' he asked.

'Scissors cut,' Ethan Shaw said as he sat down.

'Er ... Yeah,' the youth said. 'Not seen you here before,' he added as he draped a sheet across his customer's torso and lap.

No bloody wonder, Ethan Shaw thought.

'New to the area,' he said.

But he had achieved his objective. Reflected in the big mirror he now stared at not only his own image but the view behind out through the shop's front window and on to the road. A bus stop was positioned right across from the barber's and waiting at it stood a tall man with long auburn hair irritably dragging on a cigarette. Even as he watched, two shopping-bagged housewives, a gossiping pair, joined him there.

The fledgling barber clicked anxiously away. In a while the long red lozenge of a bus drew to a halt in the centre of the reflecting mirror. When it moved on it had taken the housewives with it. The tall man was still standing at the stop.

Ethan Shaw knew that only one route serviced that street. He pulled his focus back from the view over his shoulder and looked nervously at the cut-throat razor laying nakedly askew on the plastic shelf in front of him.

13

A BUS WAS DUE AT THE end of his road in six or seven minutes. He had already wrapped the Paget-Bourke portrait in a couple of towels and stuffed it under his low bed. Now he hastily rummaged a random collection of his bits and bobs – brushes, paint tubes, charcoal, pads – into his big satchel bag and shrugged on his reefer jacket. Finally, the one contrasting action precise and considered, he shoved into the jacket's right-hand pocket the Victorian clerk's ebony cylindrical ruler. If anyone should ask, it was a last minute afterthought.

He flung out of the house and across the road. Once more there was a shape in the Seat. Once more thirty paces on past the car he heard the door close behind him. So. It was his own person and not his possessions they were interested in.

He arrived at the bus stop. Three teenagers, all boys, all black, all variously occupied with earpieces and smart phones, were waiting in a group ahead of him. Seconds after he had joined them a faded, middle-aged woman took the place behind him. No sooner had she rested her half-filled Sainsbury's carrier bag on the pavement then around the corner came not a tall reddish-haired man but the same difference. Not quite so tall, but broader across the shoulders. Dark, white, early thirties.

'Not another strike on, is there?' the woman protested uselessly to the world.

'No,' he said. 'One due any minute.'

The second tail was himself talking into a mobile now.

'Ah!' the woman said as a bus turned the far corner and she stooped to pick up her carrier.

He got aboard the surprisingly empty bus. The teenagers had rushed to the rear seats. He sat amidships close to the exit doors. The dark man with wide shoulders took a seat at the front. The bus moved on again. At the next nondescript stop only one passenger got on – the reddish-brown haired man who had tailed him to the barber's. Ethan Shaw stared studiously out into the suburban evening as the man brushed past him on his way to the rear.

It was only half a dozen or so more stops to the North Greenwich station and the Jubilee Line. The bus nosed its way onwards among newly developed but already shabbily down at heel apartments on the Peninsular Estate. The tired woman got out, almost arbitrarily, it seemed, and a tired old man, his face wrinkled under a New York Yankees cap got on. Oriental, Nepalese perhaps. At a further stop two women who looked like more overnight char ladies clambered heavily on and then two younger women, slightly sleek, slightly sexy. Evening class? Down-market hen party? In the strange mix of yellow artificial light and gathering darkness it was hard to say. Within the bus everything, life itself, was on hold. Time was suspended. Ethan Shaw sat as motionless as everyone else and watched the in-bus security pictures circling around in regular turn on the screen. Neither of the two men were paying him or each other the slightest regard.

At North Greenwich time began again. Everyone got out. Ethan Shaw was the first to descend. He took his time walking to the tube's turnstiles. As he retrieved his oyster card he saw that the two heavies were now walking together in a line dead astern of him. There were more homeward bound travellers streaming past him towards the exit than opposite numbers going in to town. He maintained his leisurely pace. When the choice arrived he took the stairs down to the platform level rather than the escalator. So did the two behind.

No train, as could sometimes happen, was in and waiting. He must have just missed one. The long platform was almost deserted. He moved towards the end where the front of the train would halt and found he was glad that the state-of-the-art station design had enclosed the tracks in a plexiglass cylinder. The platform-long cylinder had sliding doors matching those of the tube train carriages. No train at rest, the outer doors were permanently closed. No suicidal jumper could jump onto live rail or beneath grinding wheels. No two strong-arm hit men could make mincemeat of a third. Not here. Not yet. He sauntered forward, circled around and back. The two had now split up again. Behind him on the long, brooding, shadowy platform they were standing about the length of a cricket pitch from each other, neither near to or that far from himself. Ah! Despite the glass cylinder he could detect a change in air pressure, could hear a remote metallic rumbling. A train was coming.

The tube whooshed and clattered into view. It duly halted with its own doors precisely opposite those of the platform. Ethan Shaw got into the all but deserted leading carriage and dumping his satchel on an empty bench seat, sat down in the next one. When he glanced up and round he saw that both men had hurried along the platform to enter the same carriage. One was sitting at its far end, the other, reading a paper now, was in the middle of the compartment and facing him. One ... Two ... Three ... there were only four other passengers along the long length of the carriage. Enough, perhaps, if it was going to take the presence of neutral witnesses to prevent push coming to shove.

Or was it? Were they at Reynold's contrivance to stop him in his tracks or was their chief objective to track where he was heading? He had thought to rejoin Ginny that evening. He had not set out to play games misleading the bad guys. But now, obviously, Hammersmith was out. Plan B time.

Canary Wharf. Bodies, faces, lined the platform and then swarmed into the carriage. Padded shoulders, white shirts, emerald fingernails. Bangkok Hermes and Lacoste. Bright eyed, bushy-tailed, fashion-conscious yuppies who had entered their kingdom and were working those extra hours to show that they were the extra. Well, welcome young pretenders, safety in numbers. He slewed his satchel on to the floor and as a slinky Arab girl most definitely not wearing a burka slid down beside him set himself to think.

Southwark came and went. By Waterloo most of the eager-beaver crowd had eased away. His two faithful followers were still, however, religiously in place. OK. he would give them a last chance.

The tube was slowing as it approached Westminster. Grabbing his satchel up from the floor he stood and moved to the single sliding door diagonally across from his seat. As the carriage shot from darkness into the light of the Westminster platform he let out a gasp of pseudo-exasperation. He looked sideways. Sure enough both his followers had also risen to their feet. He shook his head at nobody in particular and returned to his original seat. When he looked now the nearer pursuer was sitting back down as well: the further was still on his feet gratuitously taking off his blouson jacket. 'He'll have to be quick,' Ethan Shaw thought. At the next stop, Green Park, he repeated his actions and stepped out on to the platform. Yes, they had also alighted. They were following him at a slight distance as he stood on the first of the two escalators that would slowly take them all up to ground level.

Green Park was where usually when en route to see Ginny he transferred on to the Piccadilly line. Tonight required a different strategy.

He had risen to the main concourse. So, obviously, had they.

Fine. As to the manner born he went through the turnstiles and threading his way through the dozens of comers and goers headed through the direct exit to Green Park itself. Now, walking south, he had the rise of tall houses that marked the Park's eastern boundary on his left. The evening was neither chill nor sultry but, over-clouded, it was shadowy and dark with not so many other people now treading this path along its eastern edge. There were probably not too many cameras, if any, along here. Potentially he had led himself into deeper danger. But danger when a prey knows that it is hunted could be a two-edged sword. He must hope that his memory still served him well.

It had. A hundred yards or so from the station a thin alley ran at right angles from the metalled surface he was walking along and ran straight along to the tall range of terraced houses that backed on to the Park. The alley, too narrow for two people to walk along comfortably abreast, became in effect a tunnel. Burrowing forward along the boundary lines between two adjoining houses, it allowed their upper floors to arch upwards and above it. He hadn't lived long enough yet to learn what kind of fortunate individuals or institutions were able to dwell in such desirable residences, but if memory still also served, some way past the point where the alley became a tunnel it kicked sideways in a dog leg. There was a fighting chance that he could use this to advantage – fighting the operative word.

He side-stepped into the narrow alley. Nobody was walking ahead or coming towards him. Good. Now he was into the tunnel stretch. Still no-one. The narrowed, further tightened air space brought clearly to his ears the sound of footsteps closing in on him. Good.

Round the corner of the dog leg. Still no third party oncoming observer. What was page two of Unarmed Combat? 'Unlooked for counter-attack is the best form of defence!' So be it since it had to be. He unslung the satchel from his shoulder and dropped it to the ground. He pulled the hood of his training sweater up over his head. He turned on his heel and grabbing the maul stick from his jacket pocket sprinted back towards the dog leg corner.

Walking quickly the men with respectively reddish and black hair were almost at the corner themselves. At the sight of him coming on fast, halted in mid-stride, they were literally taken aback. He pressed on faster still and at the last moment his left arm crooked before him elbow out, drove crouched and sideways at the reddish, the more forward, man. Something thudded onto his left shoulder but he paid it no heed. All his concentration was on slamming the Victorian ruler as hard and as accurately as possible home across the man's leading kneecap. His aim was true. He felt as much as heard bone crack and heard as well a nano-second later a high pitched spontaneous scream echo along the tunnel.

No time to rejoice. Muscle memory staying with him from Omagh he was already pirouetting and slamming backwards hard into the second man. Simultaneously he stabbed backwards with his right elbow into the man's midriff. Bullseye! A groaning, gutteral cry had told him so and the impact had jolted his own neck tendons but Chummy at the very least was wounded out of action and was probably going to have to operate from now on with cracked ribs.

Time to spin round now, see what was in-coming. But even as he remembered the drill an unlooked for vision of delight appeared before his eyes. Floating as if in a slow-motioned dream a forearm that was not his own was gently moving across his line of sight. The hand on the end of the arm held, delicately, yes, so fastidiously, a half opened cut-throat razor. Rising in triumph Ethan Shaw stretched to his full height and – have at you, sir! – brought his solid ebony maul stick down full force on the arm's wrist bone. This time the cry was a girlish scream riding over the clattering of the razor as it skittered away down wall and along the path.

Now he could turn. The first man was sunk back against the

wall supporting himself on one leg. The second, too game for his own good, was on his knees trying to retrieve the razor. Ethan Shaw gave him a brisk back hander across the face and experienced the satisfying sensation that always arises when ebony sounds home on teeth. Now what? His luck wouldn't hold much longer. The fight had lasted no more than six or seven seconds. But in another five someone might be upon them. There wasn't time to be chivalrous. Swiftly reversing the order of assault, he struck two more blows, dazing but well short of lethal to the side of first a black haired and then a red-haired skull. One for luck time. Quickly now he ran back around the corner which – thank God! – no stranger yet approached. Re-shouldering his satchel, setting the hood free from his head he continued on to the further end of the alley. A few moments later he was in St James' Street and then, one now with occasional other pedestrians, had side-streeted his way onto the south side of a quite crowded Piccadilly.

Now ... Fortnum and Masons, no. Too late by now for Hatchard's. But further on Waterstone's. However inferior, Waterstones would still be open at this hour and serve his purpose well enough. Not feeling the least guilty, relaxing, he let the east-bound flow of pedestrians carry him along until he reached the big bookshop. After the darkness of the park, the tunnel and the side streets it seemed extravagantly bright inside.

He went upstairs to the Arts Section. The price of the heavy duty top ten collections – Rembrandt, Titian, Renoir and their ilk – so took his breath away he all but aborted his plan. Now the store seemed just plain exorbitant. But after all, he spent his life enlarging his own library courtesy of charity shop shelves. Why change his habits now? Because needs must. And over there was a 'Remainders' sign above a desk. Ah! This would do. He had found a paperback edition, thin, a monograph really, devoted to Mary Beale. It had little text but a surprisingly good standard of reproduction. He scanned the publishing details. Hmmm.

Printed in Japan. Well that explained that. And one unknown portrait painter should pay his respects to an unfairly neglected predecessor practitioner.

Paying with a credit card he purchased the book and took care to pocket the receipt. Now if CCTV put him in the Green Park area at the time of an inexplicable assault, he, the good art student, had reason to excuse his coincidental presence in the area.

He came out of the bookshop and crossed to Piccadilly's north side before turning west. Thus he descended to the Green Park station via another approach. He felt safe in resuming his journey to Hammersmith. He'd noticed no surplus of policemen asking questions in the concourse, and nobody was in sight limping along still trying to dog his footsteps.

14

IN THE WEEKS SINCE HE HAD paid it his first visit The Black Swan must have been trapped in a time warp. As he pushed his way through its doors this second time Ethan Shaw discerned the same clientele scattered in what might have been identical postures and locations the shadowy length of its long narrow bar. Certainly DI Bradley had not moved an inch. He was still on station at the far end of the counter where a more direct light set above him in the ceiling signalled out the pallor of his sandy oval face, its crinkles the more prominent as they chased his receding hair line up his scalp. He was still loyal to his no-colour suit and faded raincoat. As Ethan Shaw advanced forward he was already looking away to speak to the barman.

'Evening,' he said. 'Pint of?'

'Pint of,' Ethan Shaw nodded.

No sooner ordered than done.

'Cheers.'

'Cheers. Here's to Fulham FC.'

'Yes. Good win for them last night.'

'What we expect. Well, hope for anyway.'

'Your team, then?'

'Bred up to them. I was dragged up just round the corner from the Cottage.'

For some five minutes Ethan Shaw and DI Alec Bradley

discussed the ability of the said Fulham FC to turn it on in the last five minutes of the game and Bradley reminisced about his late father's reminiscences of Charlie Mitten.

'Mitten and George Best in their history,' Ethan Shaw said. 'There's posh for you.'

'No, that's Peterborough,' Bradley came back with quickly and with a dusty flicker of a grin. 'And I've got some good news for you. Two lots of good news, as a matter of fact.'

'Oh?'

'My respects for your not bombarding me with questions from the very moment you first walked in.'

'Everything comes. First good news?'

'Ayers is doing a runner. He's packing it all in. Off to sunny Spain.'

'How d'you learn that?'

Bradley smiled almost shyly.

'We've been paying him a visit or two lately,' he said. 'Not me personally but a team taking another look into those high class robberies I told you about – cold case wise. Pointing out the screamingly obvious. Namely that they all involve his installations. All essentially the same circuitry, same system. We kept on at his technical people – painted them into a corner. They pretty much had to admit that for the alarm to malfunction some gremlin had to be introduced upstream at their end. All they've been able to say finally is: 'We can't understand it. It's worked everywhere else.'

'Everywhere it's protecting diddly-squat.'

'Precisely.'

Bradley took a swig of bitter and looked sideways with a largely inwards smile of satisfaction.

'Doesn't take much effort,' he went on, 'to see where we were coming from. And just to keep the pressure on we've taken one of their kits away with us to see how our bright boys can make it malfunction ourselves.'

He swirled his remaining third of beer around the bottom of his glass.

'Don't truly know if it's cause and effect but Ayers has had enough.'

'Shut up shop?'

'No,' Bradley sneered. 'A creep like him will never walk away from anything empty-handed. He sold his business on to Britfast. Probably done very well out of it, I'd say.'

'Not altogether good new, then.'

Bradley shrugged.

'He's out of the body politic here,' he said. 'That's what counts. A good job jobbed. That's a result. And think what's ahead of him.'

'What is?'

'Terminal boredom. If he doesn't get caught in the crossfire of the next Spanish civil war he'll be dead inside ten years of Pina Colada and paella poisoning. And good riddance.'

'Your lads in their questioning ... They didn't come across anyone with his arm in a sling, did they?'

Bradley looked up from his glass to stare at Ethan Shaw with momentary directness.

'No,' he said. 'But there – up to a point – is my second bit of good news. As of five p.m. today there's still been no word in the Met area about any affray in or around Green Park.'

'No?'

'Not a dicky bird. Certainly no complaints. And nothing from any of the London or Home Counties' hospitals. And no leads from taxi drivers. Short to mid-term you're a lucky boy.'

'And long term?'

Turning his shoulders square on to the bar Bradley summoned the barman.

'My friend wants to buy me another pint,' he said.

'Two,' Ethan Shaw said.

They remained silent as, within earshot, the barman deftly did the business.

'Cheers.'

'Cheers.'

'The theory is,' Bradley eventually resumed, 'those two never came from Ayers. Don't be misled by the Seat. Reynolds. He set them on to you. He's not very subtle. He harbours grudges. He knows you reckon he fixed that Mini. He was looking to combine business with pleasure.'

'They weren't very good at their job.'

'They overlooked you being in the Army in Ireland. And they were being penny wise and pound foolish with that car.'

'It had English plates on.'

'False. That reg belongs to an identical right-hand model owned by a Mr Fisher in Stevenage. Totally kosher. They should have hired a Corsa or a Fiesta for their work. But they wanted to make a couple of hundred extra sovs, didn't they? Why hire when you've already got wheels? Those cracks you gave them have been treated privately. On the continent most like. Wonder what that has cost them?'

'Or Reynolds?'

'Exactly. That's where your news takes a turn for the worse. All three are now interested in payback time. The return fixture. You need seriously to watch your back. Especially with Reynolds. His type have little imagination and lots of tunnel-vision – bent tunnel-vision, if you catch my drift. To coin a phrase: they know where you live.'

'I'm only using my flat by day. Night times I'm spending with a mate.'

'Where's the mate at?'

'North London. I've been making very sure I'm not being followed.'

For a crumpled and tired man Bradley grinned almost wolfishly.

'No way they'd come in here,' he said.

*

The address which Hilary Paget-Bourke had written on the back of his Edwardianesque calling card in his elegant Edwardianesque hand was in Godolphin Square. It was there that, sensing he was playing with fire again, Ethan Shaw directed his brief letter-note.

> Dear Mr Paget-Bourke,
> As promised / threatened I am getting back to you to let you know I am close to completing the portrait. I think I can go so far as to say that the work has progressed suspiciously easily and pleasurably. Something must be wrong! I enclose a photograph of the story so far.
>
> I do, however, see the need for a tiny amount of revision, retouching. I do not possess at present a studio exactly worthy of the name or, indeed, your presence. I wonder, therefore – since so little remains doing, this should be the last session.
>
> I wonder whether I might presume to bring the portrait, myself and my materials along to your London flat and finish the job there. If this is not possible, I will, of course, make other arrangements. Please let me know.
>
> With very best wishes,
> Ethan Shaw

He only had a second class stamp but this was a Sunday so what the hell. He walked away from the pillar box faintly appalled by the finality of the envelope's disappearing through the slit and on down out of sight.

15

THE BLACK SWAN HAD BEEN A MUTED, crepuscular retreat where middle-aged men spread comfortably apart in its dimness could talk a little unofficial shop or, perhaps, when their going was unusually tough wonder out loud about the meaning of life while the rain poured down outside. The Howard Arms, by contrast this mid-week lunchtime was all heaving bustle and eyes and teeth. Positioned, snub nosed, on the tip of the peninsula created by the star-burst intersection of seven minor roads radiating out from a small roundabout mid-way between Soho and Covent Garden, it benefitted from tall, lightly glazed windows on three fronts and thus a constant flow of light. Ethan Shaw did not know the pub at all but as he held open the swing doors in the building's blunt snout to allow Virginia Faulkner to precede him he could already see from over her shoulder that the place was close to being packed out.

Mainly standing, clustered in groups of three, four or five, some thirty to forty customers, half of them female, nearly all of them a dozen years younger than the Black Swan's patrons, were filling the rough triangle formed by the Howard's converging side walls. Somehow it was brighter inside than on the street outside. Despite the press of bodies light was able to ricochet back and forth between mirrors and optics, pump handles and copper counter top. The dress code – a few padded-shouldered girls apart – was strenuously casual; jeans, t-shirts, roll-necks. Most of the girls' hair dos were brief and to the pony-tailed point. A few were stretched back from pretty faces, in what was evidently a no-nonsense workplace style.

'Follow me,' Ethan Shaw said and edged forward. There was just space enough for him to make progress. As he advanced he heard a collage of conversations overlapping from his left and right.

' ... the notice went up after the matinee.'

' ... set in concrete until the clients change their fucking three bags full minds at which moment it instantly becomes blancmange.'

' ... on this one and I'm sure we can make it permanent on those that will follow.'

' ... it's not a quart in a pint pot it's a whole fucking gallon.'

' ... he turned up more pissed this morning than yesterday. He's got to go.'

' ... keeper never had a chance. Could have gone anywhere – just happened to be a screamer.'

The bar was a semi-circle extending from the top end of the triangle. As they neared it – islands of people making amiable way for them on the whole – Ethan Shaw could see three bar staff behind the counter going like the clappers. The object of his and Ginny's expedition to the West End was not far to seek. The staff to his left and right were women.

'That's got to be him,' he said over his shoulder.

'Yup,' Ginny said.

While the subject of their attention pulled another pint, took some money, made change, Ethan Shaw studied him. The study confirmed his first impression. The man behind the bar, surprisingly young, was dark and although pale skinned had a curly bunch of semi-afro, almost gypsy hair. Otherwise, facially, he was the dead spit high-cheek boned, wide-mouthed sharp-jawed ringer of the blonde and sleekly coiffured Hilary Paget-

Bourke. If the two had once been an item, then, as with so many conventionally married couples, it must have been the narcissus thing of gravitating toward their own reflection in the other look-alike.

The change had been given. Ginny pressed forward and up to the bar.

'Stephen Saunders?' she asked.

Instantly on guard and hostile the barman looked at her as an individual person for the first time.

'Who wants to know?' he said.

'My name is Virginia Faulkner,' Ginny said. 'Angela Faulkner was my sister.'

The barman was nonplussed. His mouth opened but no words came. Ginny promptly set down on the copper counter top her photocopy of a photocopy. Inevitably the barman was drawn by her motion to scrutinise the still perfectly clear message in front of him.

'Where'd you get this?' he said guardedly as his eyes flitted to left and right.

'My sister sent me the original just before she got died,' Ginny said. 'That's to say just before she was killed.'

The barman looked straight at her again.

'Yes, my name's Saunders,' he said. 'What's this all about?'

'We've come to get you your passport back,' Ethan Shaw said.

Now Saunders was looking at him. Further down the bar someone was calling over the surrounding rhubarb babble for service.

'What have you got to do with it then?' Saunders said possessively. Aggressively.

'It's quite a long story.'

The barman picked up a cloth and wiped a counter that was already dry and spotless.

'I get off in twenty minutes,' he muttered. 'My lunch break. This place will be empty by then. You know Elsie's?'

Elsie's had turned out to be neither a pop-up health food joint nor a fast food greasy spoon but, incongruously, given its location just two minutes away from the Howard, an old fashioned meat-and-two-veg restaurant. It ran to no more than half a dozen tables. When Ethan Shaw and Virginia Faulkner came through the door they found three tables were vacant. Stephen Saunders was already seated at one of the others. He had been watching the door. His head jerk was an invitation to join him.

'Came out the pub the back way,' he said as they sat down. He looked hard at Ginny again.

'You really his late wife's sister?' he said.

'Yes.'

'What was her middle name then?'

'Two actually,' Ginny said. 'Angela Harriet Felicity.'

'What colour were her eyes?'

'Brown.'

Sauhders took that in. He was eating lamb chops. He said nothing for a moment, and then, when he went to speak again, hesitated.

'I'm sorry for your loss,' he said thickly and at last, and looked away. He was clearly embarrassed.

'Thank you,' Ginny said simply.

'I met her once, you know,' Saunders said in a voice that was still thick and low. 'I had to pretend to be his valet. For obvious reasons he wanted to keep us apart. Fool I was, I never saw it coming. Him getting married. Making out he was straight.'

A shadow had fallen across their table. Looking up and sideways Ethan Shaw saw a woman standing at its end. She was dressed in a common or garden domestic pinafore and thick-set, middle-aged, contrived to look like the quintessence of all school dinner ladies. It could only be that this was Elsie in person. Nor, given the question written all across her broad face could there be any doubt as to why she was standing there.

'Full English, please,' Ethan Shaw said promptly.

Elsie nodded and turned her head very slightly to concentrate on Ginny.

'Er ...do you think you could manage a poached egg on toast,' Ginny said.

'I'll make an effort,' Elsie said with cheerful ill humour. She went away.

'Look, obviously I'm gay,' Saunders said.

'So what?' Ginny said.

'I support Charlton Athletic,' Ethan Shaw said and was surprised to see Saunders actually grin. It was a nice smile. It brought out the boy in him.

'So many crosses in this world,' he said.

'Not at the Valley,' Ethan Shaw answered.

'The passport's no big thing any more,' Saunders said abruptly. 'It was once. I had the chance of a job abroad. But as things are I'm stuck here for ever and ever a-fucking-men.'

Virginia Faulkner looked anxiously at her partner.

'It's the principle of the thing,' she said quickly. 'Not letting you have it back – that's petty-minded.'

'Well he is, isn't he?' Saunders said chewing reflectively. 'Petty-minded. Can be. What's this about your sister being killed? I mean, that, by contrast, seems pretty far-fetched.'

'It didn't at the time,' Ethan Shaw said at once.

'And what's that supposed to mean?' Saunders said. 'You were there?'

'You could say that. Listen.'

For several minutes interrupted only by Elsie returning to bring about silence as she served a massively over-kill breakfast and a single pristine egg on toast, Ethan Shaw outlined the case against Hillary Paget-Bourke to his ex-boyfriend.

'I used to have nightmares about it,' he said and turning towards Ginny went on: 'I haven't for some time now, have I?'

Having cleared his own plate Steven Saunders nodded as he digested the inference.

'Possible,' he said. 'Although he was petty and tight a lot of the time like you wouldn't believe, he was also always going on about the great man was the man with the daring and nerve to cut through the run of the mill, small-minded little men with a bold, single decisive stroke. You know, take everyone aback and while they are dithering about crossing the Rubicon, take the high ground. Just like Hitler. The truly great man he'd say – him! the likes of him! – doesn't seize the day he seizes the hour, the minute, the split second. He was always quoting Nelson at that battle - not Trafalgar ...'

'The Nile? Copenhagen?'

'Copenhagen. When he put the telescope to his blind eye so that technically he wasn't lying when he said he couldn't see any enemy ships and went out and creamed them against orders.'

'That's sort of the conclusion we've come to,' Ginny said. 'That he was arrogant enough to place himself beyond the law. The great man pulling rank. My sister was on the point of starting divorce proceedings, you know.'

'No I didn't,' Saunders said. 'He wouldn't have liked that. Pardon me but ... he never spoke very well of her.'

'Oh it was all over between the two of them months before – Before.'

'All the same ...'

'Yes?'

Saunders nervously rearranged the knife and fork on his empty plate.

'What are you really after now?' he said. 'Revenge?'

'In a word, yes. Or to put it another way: Justice.'

'You're thinking of using my letters to shake his tree so hard its leaves will all drop off and he will be exposed?'

'Yes. It does, of course, mean exposing you at the same –'

'Oh that's not a worry. What have I got left to expose anyhow? I've done nothing illegal. Only ...'

'Yes?'

Stephen Saunders looked across at Ethan Shaw who had the feeling the barman was struggling not to blush.

'Well what you're suggesting comes very near to blackmail. Well it *is* blackmail. That's pretty cheap.'

'Petty, you might say,' Ginny said. 'Poetic justice you could also say to move on to two words.'

Again Stephen Saunders looked at Ethan Shaw.

'Perhaps ...' he said. 'Only what you should know is that back then for, oh, six months or more, I was deeply in love with that bastard. It's the only time in my life I've ever felt that way about another human being. When he first took me up – well, not at the very first – I felt that I was walking on air; that I'd come into my true inheritance. My kingdom. He was the sun I'd never felt before and he warmed and lit up everything for me. I gave up my job for him because he said he could get me something better, Instead he gave me money. I took it. What does that make me?'

There was no answer to that.

'Then he broke my heart – no, not with your sister but with some new low-life loser like me. More than one actually. I ... tried to tell myself it wouldn't go on like that for ever and then, later, that half a loaf was better than no loaf at all. But of course it did go on. And then he got to bragging about his unfaithfulnesses to me and saying that he always came home to me and if I didn't tolerate them, humour him, it was all over between us. He said that what he really liked about me was that I was so dependable ... Dependable! However far away he strayed from me, however long it took, he could always depend on my still being there when he came back to me. But I should watch my step. If I didn't tolerate all his playing away that would be it. That was so cheap itself. In the end I was the one who walked away. One day I just left Birchfield for good and all. I walked down that driveway weeping my heart out. I was 22. That's the reason he hasn't sent my passport back. He hadn't had the last word, you see. He wants to leave the door open on that possibility.'

He was talked out. He looked at the watch on his wrist just below the heart on his sleeve.

'Look,' he said, 'I've got to get back. Larry, my governor, can be a bastard too.'

He was scraping his chair back, rising to his feet.

'So what are you telling us?' Ginny said quickly.

'I'm not sure. Let me think about it. Can you come back next week?'

'I've got a job to worry about weekdays. A proper job,' Ginny said.

'Lucky you,'

'I can come back,' Ethan Shaw said. 'Right now, after that lot I could kill for a cup of tea so we'll hang on here. But any day next week, fine.'

'Come into the Howard about three next Tuesday.'

'Tuesday at three. No problem. You shoot off now and we'll pick up the tab and have a couple of cuppas.'

'That's very kind,'

Stephen Saunders nodded and went.

Ginny Faulkner looked at Ethan Shaw.

'The poor sod,' she said.

He had posted his note to Paget-Bourke on the Sunday. Since he knew Lord Popinjay already had access to it he had had no compunction about putting his true daytime address at its head. The reply was there on the communal table, hot and heavy enough, by the Friday of the same week.

Dear Mr Shaw,
Thank you so much for your little note. I am delighted to learn and indeed see that your project has gone so well. As far as I can judge from the photograph you so kindly enclosed the portrait seems quite splendid – no trace that I can make out of Picasso or Bacon!

As regards final touches – if they are as minimal as you indicate, yes, by all means bring the mountain to Mahomet if I may put it that way. I presume you will require daylight so, since it will be convenient for me, I will propose the afternoon of the 23rd next as a viable time. (It is a Sunday.) Please let me know if this sorts well with your own day by telephoning the above number.

Sincerely,
H.P-B.

What presumption in the mere initials, Ethan Shaw had to think. But that might be the least of his worries.

16

THE APARTMENT BLOCK WAS HARDLY WHAT you could call iconic. The best you could say of it was that it looked functional. Black it certainly was. Big, yet squat, long and broad rather than tall. It looked like a cube that had been pressed down from above to form an oblong. He had been vaguely aware of it for years as on his way to Loftus Road, say, or Stamford Bridge he had passed it on his right hand side as a barracks-like lump. Even more vaguely he had been aware of its louche reputation – the red topped gutter press and Bloomsburyite little magazines, had found common ground in archly insinuating that a diet of below-the-belt sex, drugs and of practices more violently sordid was the sort to which the lifestyles of the building's transient occupiers were tempted. It was a London perch, it seemed, for high-flying birds of passage – Irish MPs who were happy enough to take up their Westminster seats, Anglo-American film folk exiled to the UK for a few months on account of cheaper production costs and superior technicians, CEOs, cruelly obliged, as face-saving would have it, to work late at the office night after night. The block was a handy stone's throw from Westminster and the voting lobbies; it was minutes from Kings Road designer labels; word even ran that there was a restaurant-cum-nightclub built into the place for when such excursions might seem too wearisome or public to the residents. Outwardly the building did not suggest fast or squalid living. With its banks of flat windows flush in its flat façade it suggested nothing more racy than battery hen farming. If being fit for functional purpose was a yardstick, perhaps it was iconic after all.

Ethan Shaw had never had need to do so before but now he pulled off the Embankment and worked his way to the back of Godolphin Square. Glory be; there was an empty parking spot! He slid into it and intent on making the king's ransom in shrapnel he had compiled earlier go as far as possible, delayed spooning it into the meter until he had unloaded the clutter of gear he had been obliged to bring with him – his satchel, his paints and brushes, his field easel and, not least, the carefully wrapped and nearly completed portrait.

At his back now was what seemed to be a primary school playground and before him now rose up the back of the apartment building. Or was it the back? The design was so four-square this could almost have been the intended front. The flat, flush windows facing the Embankment had got here before him. The same minimal entrance doors were in the same corners. He found he had halted in his laden walk across the street. The design was so anonymous he might have been approaching a block in Mosul or Raqqa. For a bad moment he saw this London version cleavered in half by high explosives, interior rooms reduced to ground floor rubble, some walls no more now than brick-thin facades fronting nothing. All panes of window glass would be shattered, gaping. And where rooms did remain three-dimensional, therein behind the shattered windows would be snipers with their Kalashnikovs or, worse, their telescopic-lensed rifles. Presumably here the un-shattered, darkly louring London windows were closed only upon Glocks or Browning small arms. Well he had started, so he must continue. His self-induced hallucination juddered back into prosaic reality and he continued his walk.

There was indeed a narrow entry on the building's north-west corner. Awkwardly he pushed through the door and at once stepped through a time warp. It was the smell. Musty, damply unhealthily dust laden, the cramped pawky vestibule took him back at once to childhood visits to his Aunt Lil's flat in a pre-World War Two block in South London. He realised as he turned to the lift that he had small idea of when this building had been put up – after that war, perhaps. Just. Maybe, though, in post-war damage repair days.

To enter the lift was to intensify the step back in time. However much a high-flyer you might be, this was no way a piece of state-of-the art kit to make you upwardly mobile. It was a cupboard, an old cupboard only used to store old things. It claustrophobically reeked of discarded socks and shoes, old photographs, golf clubs, body odours, mice. Weighed down as he was his hands full, he tested it to capacity. Three baggage-less adults must have been the allowable maximum load. Somehow he contrived to press the '2' button with his elbow.

He had known to do exactly this because of his phone call of three days earlier. Having allowed 48 hours to pass after the receipt of Paget-Bourke's letter – no need to seem too keen – he had called the number indicated. Rather expecting to get through to the dead-pan, nay-saying of Reynolds, he had wondered whether to reintroduce himself or play at being anonymous. In the event he had had to do neither.

'Hello?' a voice had said after the very first ring. As much from the presumption implied by the absence of all identification as by the cut-glass two vowels, he had known immediately that he had got straight through to the man himself.

'Hilary Paget-Bourke?'

'Indeed.'

'Ethan Shaw.'

'Ah, yes.'

'I'm calling up about our meeting. The time and date you've been kind enough to suggest are ideal for me.'

'Good. It did cross my mind you might prefer to make it somewhere more central. I could probably conjure up a room at the Explorers, if it suited.'

'The Explorers?'

'One of my clubs.'

'Yes. Would the room have a window?'

'Probably not. It would almost certainly be in the basement.'

'I shouldn't think the Explorers would tolerate riff-raff of my sort – even in the basement. And I shall need natural daylight.'

'Understood. Here, then.'

'Yes. All things considered.'

'Let me give you some directions then.'

A commanding officer briefing junior personnel with perfect clarity, Hilary Paget-Bourke had proceeded to do exactly that. Now, as Ethan Shaw squeezed out of the lift he knew precisely where he was.

Windowless, the second floor corridor was underlit by too intermittently spaced low-wattage bulbs. Narrow, low ceilinged it too exhaled unsavoury, dust- laden old clothes odours the long grey length of its ongoing corridor. Visibly threadbare in some central places, the dark strip of drugget upon the floor never began to suggest red carpet treatment. This was gumshoe territory from a Hollywood B movie. On the law of averages many of the building's occupants must live here permanently but the occasional residents, the transient *pied à terre* brigade, must inhibit all effort at general improvement to a common benefit. If you don't own it, don't fix it. Occupancies, in any case, must constitute the most complexly tangled web of sub-lettings and murkily joint tenancies.

Still the CO's briefing held. The rising door numbers were guiding his steps. This was it: 213. Unlucky for some. Ethan Shaw freed his right arm so as to knock on the door.

The sound of a step. The door was swept backwards away from him and there framed before him in the flesh was not as he had half again expected, Reynolds but Hilary Paget-Bourke himself. His eyes were opening wide as they deigned to acknowledge recognition.

'Hello,' he said.

'Good afternoon.'

'You come most punctually upon your hour.'

Carefully, you poseur.

'I managed to luck into an empty parking spot.'

'Lucky indeed. Do come on inside.'

Not knowing what to expect Ethan Shaw came on into the interior of the room. What he saw with his first glance surprised and cheered him.

The apartment must have been rented unfurnished. If he had walked into it in that bare state – the door opening directly into a small sitting room – he would have been plunging into yet more of the dank dog-eared greyness of the lift and the corridor approach. But the room had been perked up. It had been cheered he saw at once by a foreground furnishing courtesy of the IKEA catalogue and the northern reaches of the Tottenham Court Road. Clean cut, straightforward examples of contemporary design had introduced brightness into the scene. A simple nest of stacking tables in, perhaps, yew. A low, self- sprung lounging chair. A Conranesque writing desk in another light wood stretched before the room's one window, crisp and invitingly functional, you could only think. The bright red fabric upholstered sofa against one side wall clearly converted to a bed. You could only wonder what stories of night time revels it could tell. In a corner, manufactured in white plastic stood a streamlined version of a Twenties tea-trolley. The lower shelf bore glasses of every size and description. The top was a miniature Manhattanesque up-thrust of every exotic spirit and liqueur bottle that a lifetime's drinking experience might recognise. It was to this status symbol that Hilary Paget- Bourke had gravitated.

'Something to drink?' he had asked.

'Thank you, no. Mustn't find my wrist all atremble.'

'Ah, indeed. Bit early in the day for me too, actually.'

Fifteen all.

'Put your stuff down on the sofa.'

Feeling the better for freeing up his hands, Ethan Shaw did just that. He carefully unwrapped its bubble-wrapped protection from the all-important portrait.

'Here,' he said, 'the story so far.'

He handed the quite large, more tall than wide, unframed portrait over to its subject. Paget-Bourke took it forward towards the window.

'Good Lord!' he said at once, 'it's excellent! Window to the soul, eh?'

For a rare instant he had spoken spontaneously. He had made no effort to exclude his surprise from the reaction. At once he attempted suave apology.

'I'm sorry,' he said. 'That must have sounded extraordinarily rude. But to be perfectly candid I hadn't dared set the bar of my hopes so very high. Your initial approach to me was so irregular I was expecting a ... well, a matchingly, er, unusual execution ... But this? ...this truly is in the grand tradition, isn't it?'

'I hope so. That was the idea.'

'No, no, you've achieved that.'

Holding the canvas at arms length and angled towards the light, Paget-Bourke was now apparently minutely examining it detail by detail. In the life, ramrod backed, perhaps an inch the taller man, he was wearing a dark brown cashmere v-necked sweater over a pale green shirt, corduroy trouser-jeans in a deep mustard shade and suede desert boots. He was every inch the gentleman at ease, the brimming over glass of casual fashion.

'I like this,' he now said. 'I really do. This is a man who is looking at his future, isn't he?'

'Where he thinks the world's going to. Certainly not to Hell in a handcart.'

'Yes. His world.'

'And, as we discussed, where he is coming from as well.'

'Yes, the playing with time thing. You know, it came off the brush so effortlessly that I'm reluctant to make changes now. You know, start with one little modification and you end up mucking about all over the place. But, studying you – as I just have been – there's still a tiny bit of retouching I think it needs.'

'Where?'

'I'd like the take the background down. The wallpaper. I'll just subdue it a bit to emphasise you in the foreground that fraction bit more.'

'I'm hardly going to object to that now, am I?'

'Then the face. I'm very happy about the way I've got the bone structure and the eyes.'

'So you should be.'

'But I'd like to deepen the hollow in the temple we can see. Just a shade. Literally. It will intensify the gaze, enhance and refine the sense of the bone-structure.'

'If you say so.'

'Finally there's the ear.'

'Oh?'

'I've rendered it too precisely. Too anatomically. Too well, if you like. It's clamouring for the viewer's attention. I'd just like to take it down a touch. Blur it slightly. We all know what ears are. Other than that ... '

'Yes?'

'Other than that little bit of 'snagging', so to speak, I'm more than happy to stand pat on that version as it is. Are you?'

'More than happy.'

'Great. I can do all that at mine. A day's work tops. I can have it back in – what? – ten days.'

'Splendid. When it arrives I can hang it in my attic and

proceed to watch the complexion deteriorate.'

'That doesn't always work.'

'What a pity. Look – you must allow me to –'

'No. No. The deal was that it was to be yours for nothing. I will photograph it for my portfolio. It will become the centrepiece. Now, what about framing?'

'Oh. I think it deserves something handsome, wouldn't you say? Something heavy-weight to link it to that past tradition. I'll take care of the framing.'

'As you wish.'

'You haven't signed it.'

'Ah ... people will know.'

Ethan Shaw turned to the sofa. The protective bubble wrap had ended draped crookedly across the unrequired rest of his paraphernalia. He took hold of its nearer corners.

'We need to protect the painting again,' he said.

'Let me help you.'

Paget-Bourke reached the portrait forward and across to allow its artist to wrap it around. The handsome features became effaced by the pimply plastic. Ethan Shaw sellotaped the edges of the wrap home again. Go for it, he thought.

'While I'm here,' he said, 'there's something else that I should run by you – something scarcely to do with the fine arts.'

'Oh?'

'It happens that in a very oblique not to mention posthumous sense you and I are going to become related.'

His hands free now as well, Hilary Paget-Bourke straightened up. It was his posture as well as the hateful glare at the back of his eyes that conveyed how much he regarded this intelligence as an impertinence.

'And how is that to be contrived?' he said flatly.

'I am about to marry your late, so to speak, sister-in-law.'

'Little Virginia,' Paget-Bourke purred. 'Well, my congratulations. When is this happy event due to take place?'

'Yet to be decided. Sooner rather than later, I should imagine.'

'Well, when it's decided upon let me make a contribution to your tottering finances. Don't waste a stamp on an invitation for me. I can quite foresee that on the date you opt for a previous engagement will regrettably preclude my attendance.'

'Already anticipated,' Ethan Shaw replied. 'After all I don't believe it's so very likely my future wife will want to see among the well-wishers the man she has no doubt murdered her sister.'

Paget-Bourke had sustained the thought of his being linked to the common herd with almost stoic indifference. Now, however, although his patrician features did not alter by so much as a twitch, the indignant glare in those eyes seemed to flare up in unmistakeable alarm.

'Virginia,' he said at last, his voice cool and steady, 'always did have a regrettable penchant for melodrama and airport paperbacks.'

'It's a belief, as it happens,' Ethan Shaw said, 'that I share.'

'And do you now?'

It was thoroughly amazing how person to person antagonism could be so immobile.

'Don't you think you're being rather rash?' Paget-Bourke said.

'It was a peculiarly tacky crime. Too much chance was built into it. That car sabotage could have created a pile-up involving half a dozen vehicles. Half a dozen lives could have been lost.'

'You will remember from the inquest that at the time it occurred I was fifty miles away or more travelling aboard an Intercity express.'

'Your type always delegates sharp-end, hands-on work to the lower classes.'

'My type. Different from yours, you think.'

'By a country mile, thank God.'

'It pleases me too. You do surely recall that, after a long and painstaking enquiry into all the pertinent facts, the inquest returned a verdict of Accidental Death. You're not so foolish as to try and have its findings set aside, are you?'

'No, I don't suppose we will attempt that. You're in a position to hire much more highly profiled mouthpieces than we could ever hope to afford. And to lunch with far more influential associates. Virginia and I have lives of our own to lead. We'll no doubt let sleeping dogs, however tacky, lie. We'll walk away and let it go.'

'Well then ...'

'It's just that we wanted you to know that we know.'

Beginning to see his way clear Hilary Paget-Bourke expressed his relief in a self-satisfying smirk.

'Thus you find it confirmed that money talks,' he said.

'And kills.'

'I do, of course, categorically deny the allegation.'

'You don't have to. I'm not wearing a wire and whatever you say, I'm never going to believe you.'

The two had been standing all but toe to toe. Now Paget-Bourke retreated a pace and pivoted through 90 degrees. His tense, affronted and wax-work like stance relaxed into a looser, more speculative posture.

'Let us suppose – just suppose – for a moment that your preposterous allegations were true,' he carefully said. 'Would the result be so outrageous?'

'How can you possibly say it wouldn't be?'

'Look at the balance, the two scales. In the one a single uncomplicated but presumptuous slit, in the other the future well-being of, what, sixty million UK souls.'

'You can't mean that.'

'But I do. Who else might deliver them from international evil?'

Realising that the man opposite to him in the Jermyn Street casuals was certifiably insane, Ethan Shaw looked at him with fresh and inward trembling.

'You?' he managed.

'Certainly. Who else in the country might grasp the nettle? Might–'

''Strike when the iron is hot ... Good God man, you lead a party of two MPs. The Independent National Party polled less than one tenth of the popular vote. Your equation is false.'

'Oh?'

'It isn't one life against sixty million: it's one against sixty million lives led by you. Sixty million saddled with you as their dictator, their Big Brother, their Head Boy. That's their only relevance in your diseased mind. They're a potential fan club for yourself. But nothing like that is ever going to happen. You are so twisted, so spoilt, you've lost all touch with reality.'

Paget-Bourke actually hissed. His ivory complexion had turned a whiter shade of pale.

'My mind is diseased?' he said tightly.

'I think it must be, yes.'

Another hiss and then a slow return to the palor of a classic antique statue.

'We had better leave it there,' Paget-Bourke said. 'You will if you know what's good for you. We are agreed, yes? Live and let live?'

'Alas, yes. Literally. We are, I hope.'

Ethan Shaw hitched the satchel's strap over his left shoulder.

'Oh,' he said. 'Except for one small detail. For too long now you've been depriving your former ... er ... associate Stephen Saunders of his passport. He'd like it returned.'

'After so long, I can hardly trouble myself with pettifogging details such as that. I don't imagine that I any longer know where his passport might be.'

'Yes you do. Just as he remembers perfectly well where he has put those letters you wrote to him when love's young dream seemed to be so true.'

'Letters?'

'Love letters. Hand-written. Straight from the heart or thereabouts.'

'What are you saying?'

'It's more a question of what these are saying.'

Taking a couple of steps sideways Ethan Shaw reached down into his satchel and brought forth a sheaf of documents enclosed in a clear plastic folder.

'So what are these?'

'Photocopies. Photocopies of photocopies. Of photocopies of originals.'

'The letters you allege exist.'

'And the rest. The other copies are largely scattered among various sets of safe hands. You know, with solicitors and such. Sealed envelopes. The to be opened in the event of a sudden death sort of touch.'

'How original.'

'Original enough. So to answer your question: to seal our 'live and let live' pact we should engineer an exchange of documents, letters for passport. All good chums again.'

'Oh really. I can deny those notelets in any court in the land.'

'Armed with the shining sword of Justice, yes. But not against the testimony of a handwriting expert.'

Ethan Shaw slipped his right arm through the strap on his still collapsed easel.

'An exchange,' he said. 'It will draw a final line under all of this. Demonstrate good faith.'

He picked up the now securely re-wrapped canvas.

'You know,' he said, 'ironically I've derived more enjoyment from working on this than from anything else I've done before. I think the contempt and disgust I feel for you freed up any inhibitions I might otherwise have had technically–'

'You're not demanding any money with your menaces ... ?'

'That would be blackmail,' Ethan Shaw said as he opened the door into the corridor. 'That's illegal.'

He paused a moment.

'An exchange,' he said. 'Nothing more. I'll be in touch.'

*

Struggling with his satchel he was no more than halfway up the garden path when the front door flew open and, more wild-eyed than he had ever seen her, Ginny stood glaring at him in her doorway.

'How did it go?' she blurted out.

'Oh, pretty well, pretty well,' he said as he swivelled the satchel back over his right hip. Almost rudely he pushed past her who was no less than his fiancée and on into the house's narrow hall. He dumped the satchel at the foot of the stairs.

'He loved the portrait,' he went on. 'The apt expression given what he is would be to say he was over the moon. He loved it. We were right. You couldn't lay it on too thick. Paint included.'

'That's not what –'

'I played right into his ego. He hasn't a clue that for anyone with two brain cells to rub together I've seen to it that he'll be hung up to dry. He's standing there with feet of clay.'

Not that he'd painted the feet. He pushed on into the living room and, feeling increasingly uncomfortable propped the bubble-wrapped portrait up on the nearer armchair. When he straightened up and turned around she was framed in the inner doorway looking daggers at him. She had every right to. She would have been worrying herself sick. He had had no right himself to come over all facetious on his return.

The curtains at either end of the long, knocked through space were drawn closed and once more the austerely grey room was trying to exclude the wearisomely troubled world outside and exude serenity but he was aware that she was still wearing the trim blouse, the thin blackish skirt she had put on that morning to go to work in and he knew that as she had gone through the routine day doing her usual bits and pieces she must have had that hell of a time. She will have spent the day dreading the worst, frantic. This moment now was as near as they had come yet to having a row.

'I'm sorry,' he said. 'I shouldn't have come in trying to be such a clever dick.'

She gave him a long level look and with it the blaze of alarm and anger faded away from her outrageously blue eyes.

'I've been scared stiff all day,' she said. 'I'm glad he liked the picture. Let's have a drink and you can tell me what I really want to know.'

She walked past him and on into the kitchen. He felt about six inches tall. When she came back she was carrying two glasses of some kind of white wine. She handed him the one.

'Thank you,' he said and knew that she knew he was not referring to the wine.

'Well?' she said.

'Er ...not totally sure,' he said. 'I let him have it with both barrels. Right between the eyes.'

'How did he take it?'

'Oh, tried to be calm and collected, doncher know. But he didn't like it one little bit. Hated it. The fact is, though, I overplayed my hand. I took my eye off the ball.'

'Oh?'

'I told him about us.'

'No!'

'Yes. I knew it would get right up his nose – him being linked to the peasantry and a low-life type like me. And it did. I swear he disliked hearing that more than being told to his face he was a murderer.'

'Well, you and I as an item would come to him as a huge surprise. He's had three years to get used to knowing he's a killer.'

'He didn't offer us any sincere congratulations.'

'Don't I know that already! He can't abide me. He knows I saw through him from the first moment I laid eyes on him. But, of course, now he knows –'

'Where I've been disappearing to. To be with you. Where the letters are.'

'You did go into the letters, didn't you?'

'Of course. They're our only bargaining chip.'

'Did it rock him – finding out we knew about them? Have them?'

'Yes. He tried to stay cool but didn't get anywhere near managing it. I reckon he was genuinely more worried about them than about the murder charge. I mean, I admitted straight out that we didn't have the fire power – the money, the know-how, the connections – to get the inquest verdict overthrown.'

'So ...?'

'I used the expression 'live and let live'. We'd stay shtum and he could have the letters back, the originals.'

'But that's insane! Suicide. Once he's got them back in his possession –'

'I know. But I was being two-faced too, wasn't I?'

She looked at him not comprehending or daring to comprehend.

'I said we'd exchange the letters for Stephen Saunders's passport. Said exchange to be arranged.'

'But meanwhile we're sitting ducks,' she said. 'Here.'

'I know,' he replied. 'I know. Is there anyone, any friend who might possibly take us in for a couple of weeks?'

She thought for a long moment. She walked to the unencumbered armchair and slowly sat down. Slowly she shook her head.

'No-one, no-one I'd care to get involved.'

'It would only be that long.'

'No.'

He grimaced, swallowed whatever was left of whatever wine it was. He stayed on his feet.

''Well it won't be nice,' he said. 'But we'll have to go into digs. Just until we can bring matters to a head.'

'It doesn't seem right, it doesn't seem fair, that we should be the ones having to go on the run.'

'It's not. But that's how the systems work. Better safe than sorry.'

'But run where?'

'The Kings Cross area,' he said quickly. 'Lots of el cheapo B&Bs around there. No better than they ought to be. Not so el cheapo either. We'll just–'

'I'll manage the money!'

'It'll be pretty grotty. Ghastly actually, but needs must!'

'They'll come here!'

'But we won't be here. Nor the letters.'

'They'll trash the place!'

He swallowed. His mouth was already dry again.

'We'll have to chance that,' he said. 'Anything valuable, precious, we can take with us. It'll probably never happen. You've got a pretty nifty alarm system.'

'I'd rather stay here.'

'No! If I could trace your address inside half an hour, how long do you think it will take Reynolds?'

'Seconds.'

'Right. What's your set-up like at work?'

'Oh that's all right. Biggish, open-plan work area. Lots of people. I'll be safe enough there. Ethan! They could come through the door here any minute!'

'No. I don't think they'll get geared up that fast. But here's what we'll do. Tomorrow you go to work exactly as usual. I'll go up to town and pound some pavements. Find us somewhere. Tonight I'll stay here. Sleep down here.'

'You can't do–'

'Yes I can. More comfortable than my pad, believe me. You can leave the heating on. Anyone comes through the door will have to get past me. Plenty of time to dial 999. Not that it'll happen.'

'Then what?'

'I'll see you here the moment you're back from work. Then a couple of grips, a taxi and we're out of here. Safe.'

'For the time being.'

'I've an idea about that.'

Later, to help restore their shattered confidence and to fortify themselves against the squalid grottiness they were about to inflict on themselves, they paid a return visit to La Bella Vista. As before the food was splendid and this time, with his eye on the immediate hours ahead, he was at pains to drink deep of a particularly strong Barolo. When they returned to the house they went upstairs for a while and then, events having taken their natural course, he got to his feet and put on his street clothes once again.

'You might just as well stay up here,' Ginny said.

'No. If – a chance in a thousand – they come, being downstairs could make the difference. You'll have time to call the police and they'll hear you at it. They won't hang about.'

'The alarm system is movement sensitive. We can't leave it on.'

'No need to. Nothing's going to happen tonight. We're over-reacting. I'll be fine.'

Armed with the duvet and blanket she had found for him he went back down to the living room. The sofa would not quite take his length. An armchair would be favourite. He settled for and in the one furthest from but facing the front window. Ah! It was softly firm. Would do a job. He scrunched back into it, a be-jeaned knight errant as warm as toast.

Now, for the second time in a short while, he was in a London suburb listening, trying not to listen, to noises in the night outside as he went to sleep. This street was quieter than the one he knew in Charlton. This grey room with its heavy curtains, its superior build, its heavier air was quieter by far than his own stuffy pad. He heard no creaking, no semi distant traffic, no heels clicking by outside.

For a while, physically comfortable, he was self-conscious and trying too hard to will himself asleep. He tried his own version of counting sheep – old film stars who had worked together, Tracey and Hepburn, Bogart and Bacall, Astaire and Rogers ...

He awoke abruptly, not through any outside disturbance but from an inner impulse. He was awake as instantly and smoothly as an expert swimmer rises naturally up through the water about him to the surface and cool air above. His eyes were wide open and not sandy with fatigue. Somehow grey light had seeped into the room. He looked at his watch. 6.20! A spasm of pleasure shot through him. 6.20. He had slept for over six hours! He had no right, no need to feel tired. He would truthfully tell himself he was wide awake.

He stretched himself straight and gave it five minutes. Not a sound from above. Gingerly, as quietly as possible, he got up from the armchair and made his way into the kitchen. As he trickled water into the kettle he heard an alarm blatt itself awake upstairs. He snapped the kettle on regardless.

17

SOMEONE HAD BEEN SO SELFISH AS to commit headlong suicide under a train at Ealing Broadway. The entire tube system was in chaos even down into central London. Ethan Shaw was obliged to wait on the increasingly over-crowded Kings Cross platform for a short eternity. He could easily have walked the distance to Seven Dials inside the time he listened to inaccurate and irrelevant public address announcements and the proliferating coughs of his fellow travellers. When he at last pushed through The Howard Arms' swing door it was chalk turned to cheese. The place was all but deserted. Stephen Saunders was sitting at one of the pub's few tables nursing what looked to be a lager. At the far end of what now seemed a strangely large and quiet room one of the barmaids from the week before was manning the curved bar at the further end.

'Sorry,' Ethan Shaw said as he slid down into the chair opposite Saunders, the Underground's all over the place.'

'Yeah, I heard,' Saunders said. 'No problem. I was always going to be here, wasn't I?'

'Are you on your break?' Ethan Shaw said.

'Properly speaking, no. But as you see there's hardly ever anyone in at this time of day.'

'Where's everyone gone? It was heaving in here last week.'

'They're all back at work. It's half an hour later now than it was then.'

'Work?'

'Stage work mainly. They're mainly all theatre people. Backstage crew. Carpenters, sparks, etc. A few actors. We're on the edge of theatreland. Lots of rehearsal rooms hereabouts. And just around the corner there's an outfit that stages Business Conferences for big companies. This place lunchtime is a Job Centre. They're all moonlighting, doubling up. In the evening they go back to their day jobs if you see what I mean.'

'Sort of. Look, before anything else, I've come with a couple of questions.'

'Yeah?'

'One: how old are you?'

'29.'

'Same age I am,' Ethan Shaw said. 'Snap. I thought, give or take, we were much of a muchness.'

'Are we? Who are you? What exactly do you do?'

'Right now I'm a student.'

'A student?'

'A mature one. Art. I'm working at being a painter. I'm doing a Fine Arts degree.'

Stephen Saunders nodded with his glass raised to his lips and sipped his beer.

'That's something worth doing,' he said.

'Well I hope so.'

'For itself, I mean.'

'I'd like to think that's true because it's probably going to make me poor for the rest of my life. What's your work history?'

This time Stephen Saunders had just taken a sizeable pull at his drink. He held up his glass to show only an inch of lager remaining.

'Look,' he said, 'I'm 29 and my glass is more than half empty.

That's appropriate. I don't really have a 'work history', do I? No more than I do a future.'

'No?'

'I was OK at school. Grammar School. I got decent A levels and so on; a place at uni.'

'Studying what?'

'Chemistry basically. Only I didn't study. That's when I ran off the rails.'

'Drugs?'

'No.'

'Why then?'

'I just couldn't cope. First time I'd been away from home ... I never knew my father, you see. He dropped dead when I was two. I had three sisters but my mother spoiled me rotten. Now suddenly I had to deal with laundry, a bank account, being on my own.'

Clearly embarrassed by these memories Stephen Saunders emptied his glass completely.

'Another one?'

'No thanks. I can help myself in a minute ... The main thing was being by myself. I could, well, explore what I was supposed to do. And be if you like. I could explore being gay. There was this bloke. The first time with him I lay there simply not knowing what I was supposed to do. Then I found out. After that it was everything – all I wanted to do. I hardly opened another book. I had exams at the end of the first year. I knew I was going to fail them. On the day I never even bothered to turn up. They threw me out. Who can blame them?'

'I know. If you don't take them no-one can say you failed them,' Ethan Shaw said.

'Right. Something like that. Only you can't succeed either, can you? Can't get on. Story of my life, really. Bollocks things up before you're put to the test.'

'So what did you do?'

'Went on the dole. Got a job I was starting to like actually – at a Garden Centre. Only carting stuff about in the main but I was beginning to relate to plants. Then the boss, a woman, a widow heard I was gay and asked me into her office for a chat. She didn't mind. She was quite grown-up actually. She said: "Do your own thing, you're entitled. Just don't bring it to work".'

'Fair enough.'

'Yes. But I was just getting involved with Hilary at that time.'

'How?'

'My local MP. I felt I was on the scrapheap long term – couldn't type, an IT idiot, didn't drive, suspiciously old for a 'junior'. I couldn't even get a job in McDonald's. I was coming round to thinking I should go back to square one. I'd written to Hilary asking if he could help me. He wrote back suggesting we meet. So we did. Ha! Love at first sight! He told me he could get me a job as a trainee paralegal with a big firm of solicitors in London. I was naive enough to believe him, of course. I stopped looking anywhere else. I went back to my lady boss and got all 'noble'. Told her she'd had no right to raise the subject of my sexuality.'

'I'd say you were right.'

'Not really. I was coming all over precious. Like some of the actors who come in here. To show how 'sincere' I was – pure – I went ahead and resigned. After all, I was going to have a white collar job, wasn't I? No more bags of compost.'

'And the rest is history.'

'It certainly fucking is.'

'Give me a minute while I get a pint. Sure you won't have the other half?'

'No thanks. Tell Maggie it's on the house.'

Ethan Shaw got to his feet and going across the almost empty bar room ordered his pint.

'On the house,' Maggie said he was reaching for his wallet. The glass was brimming. He sipped a safety margin away and then went back to the table.

'Cheers,' he said as he sat down. He drank deeply, smacked his lips.

'How did you fetch up here?' he said.

'I came to London anyway, didn't I? Under my own steam. He'd been all 'manana', hadn't he? Even before we split. But forget it! Forget London! With my background I hadn't a hope in hell of paralegal work. I tried to be a film extra – couldn't get a ticket. Did a bit of waiter work. Then I met a guy – in the usual way – who introduced me to Larry, the guv'nor here. He was looking to take on staff as cheap as possible. No insurance stamp, no minimum wage. We came to a deal.'

'Namely?'

'I get to sleep here – in the attic – for free. I get breakfast and an evening meal. Pocket money. In return I pull pints, work the barrels in the cellars, clean the pipes, clean out the loos, throw out the occasional tosser, help Larry do all the books.'

'All the books?'

'He's got three sets. One for the Revenue. One for the Brewers. One for himself so he can tell how things are really going.'

'You make me feel very naïve.'

'Bent as a corkscrew, he is. And hard with it. As you now know, this place makes its money at lunchtime. A bit of theatre audience trade in the evening. That's about it. But two, three times a year a band of very hard middle-aged men get together in here and talk and talk. Those evenings that they are here the Guinness and Paddy sales go through the roof, if you catch my drift. Now, Larry's second name is Foggarty. He makes out he was born in London but...'

'But?'

'But on the other hand he's got a gun behind the bar and I would guess at least one more upstairs.'

'What for? What's –'

'He swears blind it's in case there's big trouble here. But he never says who would be causing the trouble, sure and begorrah.'

Ethan Shaw supped some more beer and glanced thoughtfully at Maggie behind the bar. Yes, she hadn't had an accent, but she did look as if she might have been christened Caitlin. He pulled his focus back to Stephen Saunders's own eyes.

'In an ideal world,' he said, 'what would you truly like to be doing right now?'

'Retraining. Well, training obviously.'

'As what?'

'I'd like to be a landscape gardener, I reckon. I think it goes back to the Garden Centre. One day. Not that it'll happen. I'm stuck here – three years nearly I've been here now. Yes, I've a roof over my head, I know where my next meal's coming from. But it's not a life, is it? Not for ever, it's not. It's got no worth. It's got no dignity. No more either than I have. But that's what I'd like.'

'Stephen,' Ethan Shaw said gently, 'I don't think I've ever talked with anybody who, deep down, has as much dignity as you do.'

Across the table from him Stephen Saunders could not prevent a deep blush mantling the smooth white skin of his over-young face.

'Look at me,' Ethan Shaw continued, 'I futz around on a few square feet of canvas with brushes and paint. But a landscape gardener is an artist on a grand scale. He creates great prospects that endure for decades. Centuries. He creates looking into the future. I doubt if my work will ever last that long or bring anything like the same amount of pleasure into the world. But I do know about student grants. Grants for mature students. I've found out the hard way. There are all sorts of Agricultural and Horticultural training schools. Institutions. Academies. For starters it's just a case of googling a list up. If you'd allow me to, I'm sure I could pilot you on your way.'

Stephen Saunders raised his head and sat up straighter.

'Like I just said it's too late for me,' he said.

'No it's not. I'm 29 too, remember. A 29 year old is more

dedicated than a teenager. Further Education Institutions are always thrilled to discover "late-bloomers".'

The pale grey eyes of Stephen Saunders had taken on an unexpected depth and intensity.

'We're strangers,' he said. 'You'd really go out of your way to mark my card?'

'Whatever else, I'd be very happy to.'

Stephen Saunders let out his breath. He smiled. He nodded his handsome head.

'As regards whatever else,' he said, 'my answer is 'yes'.'

'With the passport?'

'Yes. It's not just blackmail. It's a matter of dignity too.'

'Exactly. Now, listen. There are one or two other things we need to sort out.'

18

ONCE AGAIN PAGET-BOURKE HAD ANSWERED THE phone immediately and in person.

'In fact,' he was now saying, 'I was able to lay my hands on the passport quite readily.'

'I thought you might be able to do that,' Ethan Shaw replied. 'Equally, I've managed to make contact with Stephen Saunders. That's why I rang. He's agreeable.'

'He may have been once. So we should meet.'

'Yes. Where are you now?'

'Birchfield Hall. But I shall be travelling up to London this afternoon and then in town for several days.'

'Right.'

'The Explorers might well suit.'

'I've already explained – not my style.'

'There'd be no problem. You would be my guest.'

'Think it through. I'm trying to do you a favour. There would be witnesses – documented paperwork. You'd have to sign me in.'

'Witnesses to what?' I might ask.

'We need somewhere neutral. Unobserved.'

'Where then?'

'Blackheath.'

'Blackheath?'

'The heath itself. In the evening. It will be deserted.'

'Oh my good Lord,' said Paget-Bourke, 'do we really have to stoop to such penny-dreadful measures?'

'Yes we do. Neither of us is travelling first class here.'

'By which you mean?'

'Listen carefully. In the north-east corner of the actual heath, at Blackheath, across from the War Memorial on that particular corner of Greenwich Park, there's –'

'Slow down, you're confusing me.'

'Treat yourself to an A-Z. The spot is off the top of a road called Maze Hill. There's neglected ground there – a place where it looks as if they once tried open cast mining for gravel. There are several biggish dips in the ground there – like over-size golf bunkers. They're overgrown with bushes and stuff. Ideal for cottaging, I'd imagine.'

'So Saunders will be with you?'

'No. He says he's no wish to meet with you again.'

'Good. Inform him the sentiment is mutual.'

'Virginia and I will meet you. We'll be waiting there. Thursday at 8.30.'

'And with the letters?'

'Yes.'

'Does Saunders want – how shall I put this? – yes, a sweetener to lubricate the transaction.'

'No. He says he just wants what is rightfully his.'

'I think it's the Foreign Secretary's property actually. How do I get there?'

'You can pick up a bus in Whitehall.'

'I don't do buses.'

'A taxi, then. Or train to Blackheath overground and then taxi.'

'Oh my Lord.'

'Less than half an hour.'

What's to prevent us using the post?'

'Your good self. Your past behaviour.'

Ethan Shaw could feel Paget-Bourke's grip tightening on his smart phone one hundred miles away.

'Very well. Thursday at 8.30. If there's a division and I can't make it I'll call this number and let you know.'

'You'll make it. No vote of yours is going to affect a thing.'

Ethan Shaw clicked off the throw-away el cheapo mobile and threw it away into the waste bin in the corner of the kitchen. He looked across the cheap formica table at Stephen Saunders.

'We're on,' he said.

19

IT WAS A WILD AND GUSTY night. The wind blowing strongly at their backs from the south had bowled them across the open heath in next to no time. Under the impersonal, enervating orange of the sodium lights on the tall lamp-posts lining the diagonal road north from the village centre they had quickly arrived at the comic-book rendezvous. The sharply cold wind had whipped at their ears. Motorists scuttling by behind yellow-bright headlamps had seemed creatures of another sort in another sort of world. Their own was not a world of nightmare but of bad cheap opera whose melodrama while failing to suspend disbelief nevertheless held you entrapped.

'This is madness,' Virginia Faulkner said yet again as the wind forced her topcoat's collar across her mouth. 'You know we can't really trust him.'

'I think we can,' Ethan Shaw said as he continued to wonder. 'I think he intends to play fair this time around. Look, there it is.'

They crossed the A2 and then a lesser but still quite busy road and thereby moved beyond the throw of the orange lighting into a murky dimness. Grass was now thick and clumpingly spongy under their feet. Moonlight came and went about them as above their heads and above the light glare countless clusters of torn grey-white clouds fled panic stricken in headlong flight before the wind. The gibbous moon had become the world's largest weather balloon as it head-butted its way through and behind the cloud wrack.

'Here,' Ethan Shaw said. 'Our Dingley Dell.'

Just a few yards beyond the last road they had reached the rim of the first scooped depression in the heathland. The latest momentary shining of the racing moon showed them a chalky, grassless trail where mountain-bikes and earlier walkers had beaten flat a footpath down into a hollow of gorse bushes and brambles.

'I'll go first,' Ethan Shaw said. 'Lean on my shoulder.'

Edging gingerly sideways he successfully negotiated the pair of them downwards to flattened ground some twenty feet below. Darkness had again snatched a broad view away from them but there was a sense of shrubs, bushes, even small trees all about the space they stood in. It was still and quiet here. The moment their heads had dipped below the rim of the hollow they had found themselves returned to peace and quiet. Traffic from here seemed much further away than they knew it to be. Moonlight returned. They could well see for a clear moment that no-one else was down there with them.

'You've only got his word for it,' Ginny said.

'It's going to be all right,' Ethan Shaw said instantly. So, she was still worried stiff about that. And with every good reason. But there was nothing he could do about it now.

Abruptly a rasp, a series of overlapping rasps from motorbikes with illegal exhausts tore the night air to shreds. A pack of bikers were accelerating by on the semi-distant A2 at sufficient illegality of speed and decibels to penetrate even as far as down to the hollow. The noise became a high-pitched whine and then took for ever to fade into a distanced silence. Then they heard a footfall. Out from between the bushes had stepped Hilary Paget-Bourke.

He was alone. He was wearing the country toff's Barbour jacket that Ethan Shaw had very briefly glimpsed what now seemed a very long time ago. In his right hand he was holding what in this varying, scudded light seemed to be black but which could have passed for a burgundy red passport.

'Ill met by moonlight, fair Virginia,' he said.

Proud, you cheapskate, Ethan Shaw thought.

'Is that the passport?' Virginia asked.

'What else, my dear?'

Holding it before him as if it were a pass Paget-Bourke stepped towards him until he stood about five yards directly opposite them.

'And the letters?' he enquired pleasantly.

Virginia Faulkner was wearing a large handbag-cum-purse over her left shoulder. She swung it round to her front and reached hastily into it with her right hand.

'Watch her hand when it comes on up,' a voice said.

A newcomer. A fourth voice. Reynold's voice. Wearing a shiny leather blouson jacket, his hands by his sides Reynolds had joined them from the same direction his employer had arrived from. He stood apart at right angles to their facing group.

'It could be holding a gun,' he redundantly finished.

Time stood still. There was now no sound of traffic at all. Ethan Shaw stood still as well. Frozen. Simultaneously his throat, his stomach and his scrotum clenched. His balls seemed to be trying to climb up into his gut. This was not how he had meant it to go.

'Don't be insulting!' Virginia Faulkner snapped out, 'that's not my style. Here!'

She drew into view a clear plastic folder. Inside, even in these conditions, a small assortment of differently sized and coloured papers could be made out.

'The bloody letters,' she said.

'Thank you,' Paget-Bourke said. He walked forward and took the folder from his former sister-in-law's hand and returned to his original position. He leafed shortly through the differingly sized pages one by one. 'Yes,' he said eventually, 'every one of them. All present and correct.'

He looked over to his left towards Reynolds and turned to face him.

'A good enough spot,' he said. 'Indeed, an ideal location. Very well, Martin, as we agreed. Take care of it.'

'Yes, like always. What else?' Reynolds said.

His right arm came up from the darkness shadowing his right leg. It was holding a gun – a hand gun with an extraordinarily long barrel. Ethan Shaw recognised the silencer at once and at that moment found himself transfixed even more rigidly by disbelieving shock. Reynolds raised the gun and pointed its long length in the direction of the facing Paget-Bourke.

'Tosser,' he said. 'More money than sense. All your life. Not able to organise a piss-up in a brewery. A total fucking liability to one and all and fucking good riddance.'

As if affected by the chill breeze he had coughed. As if to escape a spray of germs Paget-Bourke had jumped back a yard. Reynolds fired again. A deeply guttural moan emerged from Paget-Bourke's throat as his left arm went to his chest and driven back again he began to buckle at the knees. The moon chose to be cruel as well. Shining with an uninterrupted brightness it spotlighted the classic features distorted not by pain but by fearful incredulity. There was one more choking gasp and then spitting blood, twisting, Paget-Bourke fell down face forward and dead.

Ethan Shaw forced his eyes to look at Ginny. She was ashen-faced. Her mouth hung open. Though still on her feet and upright, she looked no more alive than her late relation.

'Very nice,' Reynolds now said. 'Dead before he hit the ground.' He put the silenced gun back inside his jacket. He drew his right hand out again. It was holding a second gun with an over-long barrel. Ethan Shaw heard a gasp of total alarm. It might have come from him. He could see now exactly what stolid, implacable Reynolds had in mind.

'Yes, very nice indeed,' Reynolds repeated. 'Three birds with three bullets. Well, four if you're counting. As the police will.

Blackmail victim freaks out–as they often do–and goes for a gun. Blackmailers reply in kind. Game set and a match ending in a tie. And another inquest gets it dead wrong.'

As he finished his triumphant set speech Reynolds raised the second gun and aimed it at Virginia Faulkner. In that moment with a supreme instinct Ethan Shaw wrestled free from the paralysis that had unarmed him and moved to shield her.

'Run,' he screamed.

Reynolds frowned, readjusted his aim. He fired – only somewhat in error. The second silencer had not done its job. An explosive whipcrack had over-topped the rim of the hollow and roared forth across the entire heath and torn on to flood the whole globe with its crack of doom finality. Puzzled, Reynolds peered forward at his automatic and as Ethan Shaw leapt forward to swipe it sideways from his hand also fell down dead. Doing so he had cleared the view through to the bushes immediately to his rear. Standing just in front of them and holding a third weapon in his hand, a gun that was actually still smoking, stood Stephen Saunders.

Once again Ethan Shaw became rooted to the spot. Then he heard a voice.

'God bless you.'

It was Ginny. She had her arms around him. He could put his arms around her. He did so. In that moment he knew that he held and would always hold unalloyed happiness. She knew this too. Why then was she weeping? He raised his head. Ginny wasn't weeping. It was Saunders still standing in the same place, the pewter coloured revolver pointed, huge in his hand, at the ground, he was sobbing his heart out as his shoulders heaved.

'At last!' he wailed hysterically. 'At last! Like all the other times. At last!'

Ethan Shaw forced himself away from Ginny. On legs he could just about trust he walked over to Stephen Saunders.

'What?' he barked out shortly.

'All my life,' Stephen Saunders sniffed, 'all my life when I've had things going for me, I've ruined it for myself. Now look what I've done. Why am I such a fool? It's all my own fault. Why do I have to be such a fucking loser? This time I'm finished and that's it.'

Ethan Shaw grabbed Stephen Saunders by both shoulders and shook him violently backwards and forwards. Tears and snot flew everywhere but the shoulders had stopped heaving.

'Stop playing to the gallery,' Ethan Shaw ordered. 'That gallery you've carried around all your life but isn't really there. Look on the other side.'

'I've just killed a man! They'll put me –'

'They'll do no such thing. Instead you will grow up. This has not been all your own fault. You've just saved the lives of two people who care about you. Yes, to do that you had to kill someone, true. But it was the execution of a man who had committed murder and was about to do it again. Justifiable if ever.'

'They'll still –'

'Shut up! When push came to shove you came up with the only possible goods. Horrendous goods for you, I know, but you held firm. You've saved Ginny's life and you've saved mine. I knew you had it in you. I told you I trusted you and you've proved me right. Thank God and thank you. Now we're going to have to work at getting you out of this.'

No longer shaking Stephen Saunders lifted up his head and looked at Ethan Shaw.

'How?' he said simply.

'By taking a leaf out of Reynold's own book,' Ethan Shaw said. 'Now: blow your nose. Start cleaning yourself up.'

Reaching his own handkerchief out Ethan Shaw walked over to the body of Martin Reynolds. Grimacing with distaste he reached into the leather blouson jacket and took out the first long, silenced heavy gun. He laid the one that had killed the nominal master close to the hand of that man's servant. He rose to his feet again and returned to the gaping Stephen Saunders.

'Now,' he said, 'give me that antique gun you just used.'

Robotically Saunders handed the gun across. With great care and delicacy Ethan Shaw wiped the huge revolver clean of all fingerprints. He carried it, still wrapped in the handkerchief over to Paget-Bourke's corpse and, audibly gagging took up the dead man's right hand in his own. Slowly he worked the gun back into the dead flesh. The index finger on to the trigger.

'There,' he could say at last. 'Job done.'

He retraced his steps and handed Saunders Reynold's second gun.

'We're going to have to leave Larry's gun here,' he said. 'But you can replace it in his drawer with this one. He probably won't notice for weeks. This one's a much better bit of kit anyway. Otherwise this is how it is going to go. Sooner or later this mess will be reported. The police will come. What will they find? That pile of letters for a start. Plus: one ex-copper widely known to be as bent as they come. Plus, one high-flying politico widely known by not such a small circle of his peers, I bet, to be no straighter than a Catherine wheel. What are they going to conclude? A failed blackmail attempt where both parties lost it in their panic. Oh, they may not believe that, they may wonder about entry and exit wounds. Who shot first, and so on, but it will suit both Whitehall and Scotland Yard to let as many sleeping dogs as possible lie. Someone will see it's not front page news for too long. Someone will keep it as quiet as possible and thereby gain their temporary elevation up the greasy pole.'

Ginny had managed to walk across and join the two men.

'Thanks from me too, Stevie,' she said.

Standing on tiptoe she kissed him on the cheek. She looked sideways at Ethan Shaw.

'What now?' she said.

Ethan Shaw was looking at his watch.

'Now – just to be absolutely sure – we wait three minutes to see if anyone heard the shots and comes. If anyone *does* come, we scrap the cover story and tell the absolute truth. All of us, right?'

'OK.'

'Your three minutes are starting now!'

For three centuries they waited, three minutes listening to the gathering roar of their accelerating pulses. Above them the wild moon continued ducking and diving through the racing clouds. Their hearts froze at the banshee wail of a distant, finally dying, siren. A fox barked too close for their jumping comfort. But no one came.

'Right. 58, 59, three minutes,' Ethan Shaw could finally say. 'On our bikes. First call Stephen, is to get your hands scrubbed and washed and ditch everything you're wearing. After that, we're all going to be in need of cover stories.'

At this precise moment the moon shone fully again to illuminate Ethan Shaw lifting his head, his shoulders straightening and his eyes brightening of their very own.

'Here, Stephen,' he said, 'how'd you feel about having your portrait painted?'